"What's funny?" l

with her at his sid

"Not funny funny, but cute funny. You look so damn cute with all that fuzz on your cheeks."

"You wanna feel it all over your skin, do you?" he growled, the expression in his eyes suddenly turning sultry and hot.

Colour swept up Aaradhya's face as she stopped in her tracks to stare up into his face. "Don't make promises which you can't keep," she protested.

"Kartik *Chitthaiya* is coming over for a couple of hours to keep *Ajja* company. And I don't have to go to work today."

"Advik…" She shook her head in wonder, her eyes shining.

"And my apartment is only a five-minute car ride."

"This is a damn tempting offer."

"Are you taking it?" he asked, tilting his head to one side to give her a mischievous smile.

"Try and stop me!" She hooked her arm in his as they walked towards the lift.

ABOUT THE AUTHOR

Sundari Venkatraman is an Indie Author who has 55 books to her credit—the 55th book being TINDER LOVING CARE. These books have consistently featured in the Top 100 Bestseller Lists on Amazon India, Amazon USA, Amazon UK, Amazon Canada and Amazon Australia in both romance as well as Asian Drama categories. Her latest hot romances have all been on #1 Bestseller slot in Amazon India for over a month.

The author writes romances, both contemporary and historical; as well as Indian Mythology for youngsters.

Even as a child, Sundari absolutely loved the 'lived happily ever after' syndrome and she grew up on a steady diet of fairy tales, Phantom comics and Mandrake comics. It was always about good triumphing over evil and a happy ending after the protagonists surmounted all unexpected obstacles.

Once she entered her teens, Sundari switched her loyalties from fairy tales to Mills & Boon. While she loved reading both of these, she kept visualising what would have happened if there were similar situations happening in India; to local heroes and heroines. And of course, the joy of vanquishing the ubiquitous evil villains! Her imagination soared and she happily ensconced herself in a rosy romantic cocoon for many years.

Then came the writing—a true bolt from the blue! And Sundari Venkatraman has never looked back.

Books by Sundari Venkatraman

Standalone Novels
The Malhotra Bride Meghna
The Madras Affair
An Autograph for Anjali
Twin Torment
Finding Anya
Mr. Perfect
Man Friday
Her Prince Charming
Love in Agartha
Arjun's Penance
The Floundering Author
Once Bitten Twice Lucky
Ryan Finds a Bride
Tinder Loving Care
Shaan Gets Hitched
For Better or For Worse

Collection of Shorts
Matches Made in Heaven
Tales of Sunshine

Novel Series
I *Marriages Made in India*
#1 The Runaway Bridegroom
#2 Her Smitten Husband
#3 His Drunken Wife
#4 Her Secret Husband
#5 The Casanova's Wife
#6 Her Bohemian Husband

II *The Bansal Legacy*
#1 Simha International
#2 Rose Garden International
#3 Maharaja International

III *Written in the Stars*
#1 Scorpio Superstar
#2 Leo's Desire
#3 Taurus Temptation
#4 Virgo's Krush

IV *The Thakore Royals*
#1 The Marriage Predicament
#2 Tied in Knots
#3 The Wooing of the Shrew

V *The Groom Series*
#1 Groomnapped
#2 Gobsmacked
#3 Grounded

Romantic Shorts
#1 Chahti Hoon Tumhe
#2 Beauty is but Skin Deep
#3 Madeinheaven.com
#4 An Arranged Match
#5 The Reluctant Bride
#6 Shweta ka Swayamvar
#7 Pappa's Girl
#8 Red Rose Dating Agency
#9 Rahat Mili
#10 Reema's Matchmakers
#11 The Matchmaker's Dream

Stories from Indian Mythology
I Dashavatar
MATSYA: The First Avatar
KURMA: The Second Avatar
VARAHA: The Third Avatar
NARASIMHA: The Fourth Avatar
VAMANA: The Fifth Avatar
PARASHURAMA: The Sixth Avatar

Historical Romance
I The Princess Series
#1 The Passionate Princess
#2 The Rebel Princess

Toolkit (Non-fiction)
Publishing Your Book on Amazon KDP

Tinder Loving Care

SUNDARI VENKATRAMAN

Love,
Sundari

FLAMING SUN

Notion Press Media Pvt Ltd

No. 50, Chettiyar Agaram Main Road,
Vanagaram, Chennai, Tamil Nadu – 600 095

First published by Flaming Sun 2021
Printed & Distributed by Notion Press

ISBN 978-1-68563-964-8

Cover design by: Unaiza Merchant
Beta read by: Lakshmi Ranganathan
Edited & marketed by: The Book Club

ACKNOWLEDGEMENT

Thank you so much Lakshmi. I couldn't have published this book without your timely help with the beta reading; especially considering the back and forth with the multiple timelines.

PROLOGUE

Bombay 1960

Ramani Iyer lifted his hand to hail a taxi before he noticed that another man had also done the same. The taxi driver, a *sardar*, smiled at both of them, giving a shrug, obviously having decided not to take either customer's side.

Ramani eyed the other man who appeared to be the same age as he and gave him a smile. "First time in Bombay?"

"Yes," said the other man, a scowl on his face. "And I am in a hurry. I need that taxi."

Ramani's smile got wider when he saw the other man scowling. "Where do you plan to go? By the way, I am Ramani Iyer from Madras." He brought both his hands together in a greeting, "*Namaskaram*."

"*Namaskara*!" said Bhaskar, who had just arrived in Bombay, same as Ramani. He continued to scowl, wondering whether to reveal his destination to a stranger. "I am Bhaskar Hegde from Mysore. I have to go to Matunga."

"Nice to meet you, Bhaskar Hegde. I also need to get to Matunga. Why don't we share the taxi?"

The fierceness of Bhaskar's scowl reduced when he realised that he could split the taxi fare with the other man. "Let's do that," he agreed.

Ramani nodded his head happily, turning to the driver and gesturing to him to open the boot.

The *sardarji* got down from the cab to open the storage compartment. "Are you both new to Bombay?" he asked in Hindi, even as the two men placed their metal trunks side by side inside the boot.

His customers looked at each other before shaking their heads at him, unable to understand his words.

The driver laughed. "I suppose you are." He shut the trunk of his taxi and waited for the two men to settle down in the back seat before taking his place in the front. "Matunga, where?" he asked in broken English, lifting his hand to gesture wildly.

Ramani and Bhaskar spoke together, "Concerns." They turned to look at each other and laughed. It looked like they were both going to live in the same place.

"*Chai*?" asked the *sardarji* in a friendly manner. After all, it was a long way from VT station to Matunga by road.

"*Kaapi*," said the newfound friends, once again together before they burst out laughing, at least Ramani laughed out loud while Bhaskar's laugh was subdued.

The driver shook his head, a wide smile on his face. "Coffee, Matunga," he insisted. "*Chai*, Masjid Bunder. Nice." He brought his thumb and forefinger together to show them what he meant.

Bhaskar looked at Ramani and grimaced. His family were particular that fresh coffee beans were bought from Coorg and roasted evenly at home. His mother, under his grandmother's eagle eye, ground the roasted beans to powder that had to be just the right texture and not too fine. This was done every day using a small black iron contraption fixed to a wooden pillar in their kitchen. His mother fed a handful of the blackened coffee beans into the top and rotated the handle while the powder was caught in a brass bowl.

The aroma of coffee powder permeated the room early in the mornings, the perfect smell to wake up to. Even as a child, Bhaskar had been fascinated with the kitchen, helping his mother with the cooking whenever he got a chance. He didn't much care for the time he spent at school, taking away precious hours that could be spent in the kitchen, learning from not just his mother, but his grandmother too.

Ramani grinned now, a devil-may-care look in his black eyes. While he loved his morning cup of coffee, he was curious to discover the taste of tea. He raised an eyebrow at Bhaskar, saying, "Why don't we give it a try?" On seeing his new friend's reluctant nod, he tapped the taxi driver on his shoulder and said, "*Chai*."

The *sardar* said, "*Balle balle*," before turning his cab into a small side street to stop at a minuscule shop from which steam was emanating steadily.

The three men got out and walked to the shop where the taxi driver ordered three cups of tea.

Ramani watched on in amusement as Bhaskar wrinkled his nose when he took a small sip from his glass. "So, what do you think?" he asked.

Bhaskar nodded. "Not bad at all. Actually, I must say that it's good, though not as good as coffee."

Ramani threw back his head and laughed. Sipping from his own glass, he found that he liked the taste a lot. Bringing his thumb and forefinger together, he turned to the *sardar* and said, "Good."

They paid the *chaiwala* before getting back into the taxi and going off in their direction. "I agree that it might not be as good as coffee, but I must say that tea is a good pick-me-up this early in the morning. Don't you think so?" asked Ramani.

"I suppose." In a much better frame of mind by now, Bhaskar asked the other man, "Have you got a new job here? Or are you on holiday?"

"Neither," said Ramani, shaking his head. "I'm going to look for a job. And you?"

"I'm also going to look for a job. I hear that Bombay is the place for new opportunities. And I am one of the best cooks in my part of the town," said Bhaskar, quiet pride in his face.

Ramani's eyes went wide in disbelief. Imagine that! "Are you saying that you are a cook?"

Bhaskar frowned, taking offense instantaneously. "Why? Is there something wrong with being a cook?" he asked belligerently.

Ramani shook his dark head vigorously. "Not at all. It's just that, I'm also the best cook in my part of Madras."

Bhaskar's jaw dropped in astonishment.

In the end, both friends managed to get jobs at Rama Boarding within a week, though as assistants of assistant to the head cook. They had both been confident that with their kind of skills, they would have been hired as head cooks.

But it was a job and both were hard-working young men. They also got to learn to make a couple of new things that weren't made at home, *rotis* and *puris*.

After three months of hard work, the bold and outspoken Ramani set up a meeting with their boss one Monday morning, their weekly day off. "Sir, I have an idea."

Ramachandra Sharma gave the young man a stern look. He had noticed that the lad of twenty-four, though hard-working, also had an ambitious streak in him. "What is it?" he asked, his voice a discouraging growl.

"We are only serving lunch and dinner here. What if we also served breakfast in the mornings and tiffin in the evenings?" asked Ramani in one breath, before he lost his confidence at the impatient look on his employer's face.

Sharma laughed sarcastically. "Is that all you have learned here, my boy? Everyone is so busy from five in the morning till past midnight, preparing the meals. Where is the place and manpower to provide two more meals? And why do you ask? Don't you like your work here?" His dark and bushy eyebrows lifted up on his forehead, drawing attention to his receding hairline.

Ramani shook his head vigorously. "I love working here, sir," he lied through his gritted teeth. "It's just that I got this idea…"

"You are paid to listen to your superiors, not to think of stupid ideas. Now go and enjoy your holiday before I come up with some more work for you to do."

Ramani rushed away from Ramachandra Sharma's presence, having lost his smile.

Bhaskar gave his friend a deep look, startled to see the serious expression on his face. He had never seen Ramani without a smile on his face. "Is something wrong?" he asked now.

"You come along with me. We need to talk." Ramani rushed down the staircase, taking the steps two at a time.

The friends walked swiftly and reached King's Circle. They settled down on the grass before Ramani spoke. He had been fuming all through the ten minutes it had taken them to reach the circular garden in the middle of the crossroads. "Are you happy with your job, Bhaskar?" he asked, looking at his friend with his sharp gaze.

"Why do you ask?" Bhaskar wasn't one to share his deeper most thoughts and feelings easily. He simply hated his job and had been biding his time before doing something about it.

Ramani picked up a small stone that had been lying amidst the grass and lifted his arm to throw it as far away as he could, hoping to rid himself of the frustration that ate into him. "Because I'm not. This is not what I imagined that I would be doing, day after day. It's been three months, Bhaskar. We are little more than waiters at the hotel."

Bhaskar nodded his head slowly. He couldn't help but agree with his friend. "But what can we do about it?" He suddenly opened up. "My father was dead set against my coming to Bombay. He told me that I should set up a small hotel locally and was even ready to invest money in it." A deep sigh shuddered through him before he continued, "I can't even tell them back home what I am doing for a living." His family was from the upper middle class and were well respected. Bhaskar wouldn't ever admit to them that he was holding such a menial position at the boarding hotel.

Ramani sat up straight. "Glad to hear that. I've been thinking long and hard. Instead of wasting our lives away like this, why don't you and I start our own hotel? We can have a combination of items from both Madras and Mysore. Can you imagine? We will be our own bosses."

A small spark of excitement pierced through Bhaskar's heart. Was what Ramani said possible? But wouldn't that require a lot of investment? He was too proud to ask his father for more money. "Er… I…"

Ramani was on his knees by now, a hand on his friend's shoulder as he bubbled with enthusiasm. "What's to stop us, Bhaskar? Just think about it. We can get a smaller place to begin with. You take care of the Kannada dishes while I will make the Tamil food. It will be as easy as pie."

Bhaskar looked up at the intense expression on Ramani's face. Could they make it work? And how much money would they need? He had an over cautious nature and was a tad wary about setting up on his own, even though it seemed like he would have an equally interested partner. "We will need a lot of money for that, Ramani. And what if we make a loss?"

Ramani shook his head, a wild grin on his handsome face, his teeth shining a bright white in the mid-morning sunlight. "What do you think of your cooking skills?" he challenged.

A look of pride appeared on Bhaskar's face, his deep brown eyes brightening up. "I'm the best in my part of Mysore," he said in a firm voice.

Ramani laughed gleefully. "Do you plan to be second best in Matunga?" he asked, "I don't mind taking first place."

"You are on. Be warned though. I'm the best. You are welcome to be a close second though."

The friends rolled on the grass, laughing, their confidence restored by their camaraderie as well as their faith in their cooking skills.

And that's how Madras Meals was started in September 1960 in a small three hundred square feet space on the ground floor of a building just half a kilometre away from Matunga station. The choice of name hadn't been too difficult to arrive at since the idea had originated from the partner from Madras. The friends managed the kitchen and the cashbox between the two of them. Hard work never fazed them as they sweated it out, serving the customers. To begin with, they hired two men to help them with the serving and cleaning.

Soon, they were going to celebrate the first anniversary of Madras Meals. It was past eleven on a Saturday night when Ramani enthusiastically wrote the next day's menu on the black board behind the cash counter:

Breakfast (From 5 am – 10 am)

Pongal, idli, vadai, masala dosai, upma, pesarattu

Lunch – *Ilai saapadu*

(served on banana leaf from 11.30 am – 2.30 pm)

Kadle manoli, parangi kootu, brinjal sambar, Mysore rasam, cucumber raita, fried pappadam, gulab jamoon, rice, chappathi

Evening tiffin (From 4 pm – 6.30 pm)

Plantain bhajji, onion pakoda, Mysore bonda, rava idli

Dinner – *Ilai saapadu* (From 7 pm – 9.30 pm)

Bisi bele rice, coconut rice, curd rice, fried vadaam, lemon pickle

He stood back to admire his handiwork when Bhaskar walked out of the kitchen, his eyes drawn to the board. "I was thinking that since it's Sunday tomorrow, why don't we serve them *chiroti* instead of *gulab jamoon*?" he asked, a rare look of mischief on his face.

Ramani swung around to stare at his partner. "You are joking. It's difficult to get the right consistency for *chiroti* and it can be a total flop if even a small percentage goes wrong. And, Bhaskar, you know very well that we get at least a hundred and fifty people for Sunday lunch. How do you think we can perform this miracle?" He was half sarcastic as he queried of his friend.

"What if I tell you that two hundred *chiroti* pieces are already prepared and are cooling in the kitchen as we talk? I didn't want to simply sit and twiddle my thumbs while you balanced this month's accounts."

A whiz with numbers, it had fallen to Ramani's lot to keep accounts while Bhaskar had taken seventy-five percent charge of the kitchen. It worked well for both of them, with Ramani still managing to cook some of his favourite dishes while also enjoying the challenge of keeping their business in the black. At the end of it all, it hadn't been too difficult as more and more people moved into Bombay from the south of India, the need for South Indian food increasing day by day. In fact, many of the Gujarati community who lived around the area had also become their regular customers, especially during the weekends.

Ramani's dark gaze shone with excitement. "Now this I must taste," he said, walking into the kitchen. He was dazed when he saw the trays and trays of *chiroti* cooling under the fan. He turned to look at Bhaskar and said in a whisper, "Now I have to admit that you are the best cook, my friend."

From Ramani, who was an excellent cook, it was high praise indeed. Colour running up his dark face, Bhaskar took a plate and served the *chiroti* on it, breaking it into pieces, before dusting cardamom flavoured castor sugar on it before pouring some almond flavoured milk over it. After adding a spoon, he presented the plate to his partner with a flourish.

"Taste this first and then talk," he said, his voice gruff with emotion.

Ramani took a spoonful of the crumbling *chiroti* along with the flavourful milk and tasted it, shutting his eyes to experience the taste. "Mmm…" he almost moaned in delight, "this is too delicious, Bhaskar." He opened his eyes to look at his friend. "You truly are an expert."

Bhaskar gave his partner his widest smile yet as he lapped up the compliment, watching Ramani gobble up the rest of the dessert with relish.

1

The apartment door opened almost immediately after Aaradhya rang the bell and her aunt, Janani, stood at the entrance with a welcoming smile on her glowing face.

"Hi Janani *Athai*, how are you?" Aaradhya greeted her paternal aunt with great enthusiasm, hugging her close.

Both women were of similar height and with slim figures. Even their facial features matched to a great extent, their eyes big and dark, sparkling with mischief. The only difference was in their age. While Aaradhya was twenty-three years old, her aunt was forty-one; and a spinster at that.

"I am all fine, Aara," said Janani, pressing her cheek to her niece's. "I'm thrilled to have you back home after… what? Two whole years?" Janani moved back to study her niece from the top of her sleek dark head to the tips of her painted toes. "You are looking gorgeous; I mean, more than ever."

"*Athai*!" Aaradhya reached forward to kiss her aunt on her cheek before stepping into the living room of the luxurious apartment in Matunga East, not far from the *Bajana Samaaj*. Janani lived in the penthouse—the twentieth floor of the building called Trishanku—while Aaradhya stayed with her grandparents on the seventeenth. "Not really. Just one year and seven months."

Janani grinned, gently pushing her niece down onto the plush sofa before plopping down next to the younger woman. "So, how was it? Playing chef at all those *firangi* restaurants? Was it fun? Or did they treat you like a brown slave? Tell me everything."

Aaradhya laughed, the tinkling sound like that of a musical fountain. "Brown slave! Isn't that kind of melodramatic? Which century do you live in, my dear aunty?" she guffawed, holding her sides as her whole body shook with mirth.

Unfazed, Janani laughed right back. Shrugging, she asked, "You mean the whites have begun to treat us as equals?" a shapely eyebrow up in query. She had a quirky sense of humour and enjoyed chatting with her niece.

Aaradhya shook her head. "I didn't face any such issues, *Athai*. So! How is the artwork coming along? How many paintings have you done during my absence?"

Janani was an artist and captured nature so beautifully in her watercolours. A graduate from JJ School of Arts, she followed her passion with zest. Her paintings were in demand, with her agent setting up exhibitions all over India. And so far, he had refused a dozen invitations from galleries based in the USA and Europe. All because Janani had not got an opportunity to put together enough number of paintings for a show abroad. Some of them got sold even before they were completed.

Janani shrugged again. "Loads, I think."

"Do you have anything to show me?" asked Aaradhya, jumping to her feet.

"Come along," invited Janani, getting up to walk to the back of her apartment, into a room that ran across the length of the house, the east-facing wall one long sheet of floor length windows. It was actually three bedrooms knocked together into one long art gallery.

Breeze blew into the room, bringing a smile to Aaradhya's face, as she looked to her left and then to her right, her eyes alight with curiosity, her head swinging this way and that as she tried to take in the number of easels which held partly painted canvases. Quickly counting, she said, "There are seven in the making."

Janani grinned. "That's right."

Aaradhya walked to the left and studied the canvases one by one, her eyes shining with joy. She loved not just the colours, but the sure strokes which seemed to light up each canvas, making it glow. "You're too damn talented, *Athai*!"

A wash of colour ran up Janani's face when she heard her niece's wholesome praise. "And for that, I'll let you choose one canvas for yourself."

"Ooh!" Aaradhya pranced about the room, checking each canvas minutely before she came across the one with a peacock in the middle of a forest. Only the peacock was completed, while a light pencil sketch of the surroundings had been done. The brilliance of the blue-green bird had been captured so perfectly in the painting. Its feathers were open and it looked as if it might begin to dance any moment. "This is mine," declared Aaradhya, touching her index finger to the perfectly painted beak of the bird.

"Done!"

"And here you go, this is what I got for you from Switzerland." Aaradhya opened the tote bag she was still wearing on her shoulder and removed a gift parcel that was eight by three inches long. "I know you'll love it," she insisted confidently.

Janani opened the parcel quickly and her mouth fell open in awe as she stared at the oil painting of the Swiss Alps, the blues and greens shimmering along with the white of the snow-capped mountain range. Her eyes quickly checking the name of the artist, she asked, "Paulo? I haven't heard the name before. But this is truly beautiful."

Aaradhya was thrilled to hear her aunt's words. "He's a local artist who is still making a name for himself. I got it for a steal." After all, she knew how expensive Janani's paintings were, the rate going up even as the demand for them increased.

"Thank you, love. You are so good to me."

"Meh! You know me better than that." Aaradhya hooked her arm with Janani's as they walked over to the kitchen off the living room. "So, what is there for lunch? I'm starving."

"Aren't you, always?! One would think you were still a growing kid."

Aaradhya pouted, walking over to the gas stove and opening the lids of the serving bowls to check what was on offer. "*Vendakkai more kuzhambu, beans paruppusili, tomato rasam* and *javarisi payasam*. Yummy! You are the best, *Athai*! You remembered all my favourites." She turned around to gush at Janani.

"Of course I did, kid. And I was sure you must be dying to eat a proper Tamil meal after being abroad for this long."

"Tell me about it." Aaradhya quickly helped her aunt carry the bowls over to the dining nook at the other end of the kitchen, before placing two circular steel plates and serving spoons on the table. "*Amma* got the cook to make *sambar* and different South Indian veggies, but I love these the best." Her parents, Vaibhavi and Kumar, lived on the nineteenth floor. While they would have preferred their only child to live with them, Aaradhya chose to live with her grandparents.

Janani watched her niece tuck into the lunch, helping herself to two portions of each item and smiled lovingly at the younger woman. "Where do you put all of it?" she teased.

"Very funny! Same as where you put yours," said Aaradhya cheekily. She was only too glad that she had taken after her aunt, in fact, her father's side of the family in the figure department. Her own mother, Vaibhavi, tended towards plumpness, how much ever she jogged on her treadmill every day.

As for her father, Kumar, he was lean to the point of being slim, even if he spent most of his time at the family restaurant, on his toes. But then, Kumar did not believe in taking siestas and preferred walking around to using his car unless he had to travel long distances.

As for Aaradhya, she loved to swim every day in the private pool that belonged to the Iyer family on the terrace of Trishanku, the building they lived in, where they also owned the top four floors along with the terrace. Either that, or she jogged for seven to eight kilometres. And at the end of the day, she was but walking in her favourite aunt's footsteps as Janani also followed the same activities to keep fit.

"So! What all did you learn abroad?"

"All kinds of European cuisine. But more than all that, I learned to bake, *Athai*. I love that part of cooking, I swear."

"When do I get to sample your baking? I want chocolate cake, like NOW. Be warned!" Janani sipped from her tumbler of water as she pinned her niece with her dark gaze.

"Tonight?"

Janani's eyes went wide with surprise. "That's nice. Don't tell me you have already baked the cake?"

Aaradhya's eyes danced with mischief. "I am telling you nothing, except for the fact that *Thatha* is even more desperate than you to taste my cake."

Janani burst out laughing. Ramani Iyer, her own father and Aaradhya's grandfather, was a foodie through and through. And he had a terrible weakness for desserts, especially anything chocolate flavoured. "I think I'll invite myself for dinner on the seventeenth floor."

"Do that! I can be your messenger and tell *Paati,* if you want." At seventy-four, Savitri still loved to make all the meals in her kitchen. Her husband, Ramani, was the first one to admit that his wife was the best cook he knew. And that was praise indeed, as Ramani's role as a chef in his restaurant was a renowned one.

In another part of Matunga, it was lunchtime at Mysuru Ahara, an extremely busy restaurant serving Kannada cuisine, in one of the by-lanes off Matunga Station. This belonged to the Hegde family and at that time, it was Kartik Hegde, second-generation owner, who was at the billing counter.

Advik walked into the restaurant, his gaze running over the two-hundred-odd seating, not at all surprised to find the place filled to overflowing. In fact, there were at least fifteen customers waiting outside for tables to empty so that they could have lunch. After all, wasn't it one of the most popular restaurants in the area? Most of the office goers and shopkeepers had, not just their breakfast and lunch, but even an evening snack at the popular restaurant that served authentic food from Karnataka. The spicy and delicious *thali*—whole meal served on a plate or banana leaf as per the customer's preference—was the most in demand during the lunch rush hour.

His eyes alighting on his paternal uncle at the billing counter, he swiftly navigated between the tables and reached the counter that was on the left, not far from the wash basin. "Hello, Kartik *Chitthaiya*!"

"Hey!" Kartik lifted his head from the billing machine to look at his strapping nephew, a broad smile breaking out on his serious face. "Advik, what a surprise!"

Advik grinned, bumping a fist with his uncle. "I'm hungry. Do you wanna join me for lunch?"

"You want to eat here?" asked Kartik, surprise on his face. Advik was fond of all kinds of food and preferred to eat a different cuisine every day.

Advik laughed. "Why not? It has been a really long time since I tasted Kannada fare."

"That's fine then. Why don't you get a table? I'll join you in a minute." He turned to catch the eye of the hotel manager who was supervising the orders. "Dayaram, come here," he called out softly, his hand gesture beckoning the other man.

When the manager went to him, Kartik said, "You man the counter. I am off to have lunch."

"Kartik Sir, there is no vacant table. Let me go see…"

Kartik shook his head. "No worries. See there?" He pointed a finger in the direction of a table in the opposite corner of the room. "Advik has already found a table. I'll join him."

"Oh!" Dayaram stared in surprise at the young man. While Advik belonged to the Hegde family, it had been some years since the young man stepped inside the family restaurant. He had heard vague stories of Advik's tussle with his grandfather Bhaskar Hegde, the head of the family who owned the restaurant. His gaze was curious as he watched Kartik join his nephew at the table for two.

"So, what have you decided?" asked Kartik, munching on a fried *papad* even as he sipped on the *rasam* flavoured with tomatoes and coriander along with a dash of pepper. His nephew had returned from the US only last week. He had been studying at the Institute of Culinary Education (ICE), New York, before receiving hands on training at a few hotels across America and the continent.

The head of the family—Kartik's father and Advik's grandfather—Bhaskar Hegde, had refused to take his grandson back into the family home, much to everyone else's anguish. But nothing could budge the patriarch once he made a decision. Bhaskar would rather perish in hell than go back on his decisions, however unreasonable they were. But neither uncle nor nephew were keen to talk about the fall out between grandfather and grandson.

"I have taken a job with the Hot Foods chain, as a chef and manager. I get to work in all the departments of the multiple branches of their eight brands." Advik almost burst out with his answer, unable to contain his excitement. It was truly a feather in his cap that they had given him this opportunity at such a young age. After all, he was only twenty-eight, though he had a couple of years of experience abroad. But then, his grades were exemplary and all his professors from ICE had given him written recommendations which were proof of his capabilities.

Kartik stared at his nephew, aghast! His eyes almost popping out of his forehead, he asked, "Are you serious?"

Advik gave his uncle a mischievous grin. "Why do you ask that, *Chitthaiya*? You surely don't think I'll joke about my future."

"But… but your Bhaskar *Ajja* is already so angry with you. How can you…?"

Advik took his uncle's hand in both of his, speaking earnestly, "Listen, *Chitthaiya*. I love my *Ajja*. And I agree that he has set up a fabulous restaurant right here in the heart of Mumbai." He turned his head to look around the crowded restaurant, people walking in and out as tables were cleaned and more customers filed in. "And yes, Mysuru Ahara is making fantastic money. But tell me something, where is the challenge for me in this?" Advik's grandfather, Bhaskar Hegde, his father, Ganesh Hegde; and his uncle, Kartik Hegde, managed the kitchen and business between them. Over and above all that, they had Dayaram to manage the business when one of the three needed a break. There were three cooks who handled the kitchen. Advik had thought long and hard, over the past few years, in fact, before deciding the course of his future.

Kartik's lips turned down at the corners as he looked at his hand enfolded between Advik's. Shaking his head slowly from side to side, he spoke in a low voice. "But is this how you envisage your future?

Working for someone else? Don't you want to have your own business?"

"Of course I do, *Chitthaiya*. And I will do exactly that in the near future. What I need to learn is all about the running of a modern restaurant, catering to the palate of the younger generation. You must agree that it's way different from what we have here. Okay!" He lifted a hand to stop Kartik from bursting out. "Let me make myself clear. I am not saying that youngsters don't enjoy our food. But take me for example. I want to eat this food maybe once in a month or two. But after that, I want to taste every damn thing from around the world. I..."

It was Kartik's turn to lift a hand to stop Advik from continuing. "I see it as a major risk, Advik. How do you plan to raise capital? How will you manage?"

Advik laughed softly. "Come on, *Chitthaiya*. Have you so easily forgotten how your father, Bhaskar Hegde, came to Bombay all those years ago, and set up on his own? Well, his blood runs in my veins too. I can and I will manage, only too well," he responded, total confidence in his young voice.

"I envy you your confidence, son. I truly do!" said Kartik, a heavy sigh shuddering forth from within him. If he had had his nephew's guts, he would have been a free bird too, marrying the woman he loved, and setting out on his own. But alas, that had been Kartik's weak point, unable to shift away from under his father's shadow.

"Do you remember what I mentioned before I left for the US, *Chitthaiya*? Will you be interested in joining me when I set up a restaurant of my own?" asked Advik softly, a gentle expression in his brown gaze. He knew the story only too well of his uncle's lost love. "You can choose to take whatever position you want," he offered.

Kartik's dull gaze lit up as he looked up into his nephew's face. Of course, he remembered Advik's words before he left for his sojourn abroad. But Kartik hadn't taken him too seriously then. "Do you really mean it? Be warned! I won't let you forget your promise. You know I am a desperate man." He was too anxious to escape his father's stranglehold on him, but having no way to actually do so.

"I won't forget, *Chitthaiya*. Give me just one year. I'll pull you out of the mess you are in. And that's a promise."

Kartik sat back in his chair, the half-eaten food on his plate forgotten; his heart beating like a drum. Was it possible for his life to change for the better? And will Janani forgive him for ditching her all those years ago? It all sounded too good to be true.

2

Aaradhya was working on her laptop, planning her days over the next week when her phone pinged. Distracted, she checked it to see that it was a message from her friend Neeti. They set up a plan to meet the next day before Aaradhya got back to her laptop. Only to find that she was in no mood to continue with her work.

Excusing herself as it was past midnight, she shut her computer to get up and stretch her arms over her head. *Should I go for a swim?* Putting her thoughts into action, she quickly changed out of her cotton pyjama set into a one-piece swimsuit of a dramatic red and black colour combination, grabbed a towel from her bathroom shelf and took the private lift to the terrace.

Sighing with pleasure as she felt a strong breeze blowing across the terrace, Aaradhya stepped out of her rubber chappals; leaving her towel on a wooden pool chair before jumping in at the deep end of the rectangular pool. Swimming up and down the length of the pool, she ruminated over her meeting with the handsome stranger at the Delhi airport.

They had both arrived by the same KLM flight from Amsterdam. She had spent her time sightseeing for two whole weeks in Europe after completing all her projects in Switzerland before taking the flight back to Mumbai, via Delhi. The extremely good looking Advik had caught the same flight that connected him from New York to Delhi, with a stopover in the Netherlands capital.

As they sat next to each other in the business class, Aaradhya couldn't help checking out his handsome profile in the pretext of looking outside the window which was on his side.

"Do you want to sit next to the window?" he asked, startling her into sitting up straight.

What a bloody sexy baritone! Her heart catapulted the first time she heard his voice, the sound striking all the right chords in her. "Don't you want to?" *After all, why take a window seat if one didn't want to look outside?*

He grimaced, his mouth pulling down at the corners, dragging the handlebar moustache along with it. "I'm going to sleep till we touch down at Delhi. So!" He shrugged, inadvertently drawing her gaze to his broad shoulders encased in a dark grey pullover, the material stretching across the contours of his chest as if it had been exclusively created for him.

With a great effort, she took a deep breath to drag her thoughts back to the matter at hand. "In that case, yes. I'd love to," said Aaradhya, unbuckling her seatbelt to get up.

He did the same before moving out of his place, waited for her to sit before settling down in her seat.

"I'll wish you good night then," he said before pushing the lever to stretch his seat out into a bed.

"Good night," responded Aaradhya, her voice hoarse as it came out of a dry throat. *That was it! A hello and a goodnight. What a shame!*

It was an effort to pull her gaze from his face that was partly covered by a blue eye mask with the letters KLM printed across in white. She stared helplessly at his lips, the thin upper one framed by the moustache while the broad lower one was eminently kissable. A tad dark, as if he smoked, they were too damn attractive. With a soft sigh that shook her slender frame, Aaradhya finally succeeded in turning her head to look out of the window at the blue sky stretching across, with small puffy clouds floating around. It was still light and she loved to gaze at the setting sun's golden rays play hide and seek with the clouds. As for the man in the seat next to her, he was a stranger while she was no voyeur.

Once they got off the flight, Aaradhya was thrilled to note that they were to continue to travel together; on the same flight from Delhi to Mumbai, this time via Indigo Airlines. Surely, he must have rested enough by now! But the man didn't seem prone to conversation as he walked in the queue, his eyes on his phone as he stood three people behind her in the line.

Just when she reached the check-in counter, a crew member from Indigo Airlines approached her. "Ma'am! I have a request. Could you give me a minute, please?"

Aaradhya turned to look at the crew member before turning towards the counter. One more minute and she would have been checked in.

"Ma'am, please. I need to speak to you before you check in." His voice was pleading by now. "There is this couple, both senior citizens. They need to reach Mumbai urgently or the man will miss his appointment with his heart specialist. Will it be possible for you to take the next flight?"

A small scowl pleated Aaradhya's shapely eyebrows. It looked like an emergency. But then, hers was only one seat. "You did say a couple, right? What about the second seat?" she asked the man.

"I can give up my seat too," called out the stranger's voice; the same one with the sexy baritone; the one who had taken the KLM flight with her to Delhi.

The crew member looked up to smile at the stranger. "Could you do that, sir? That would surely be helpful. Thank you so much. I'll book you both in the next available flight. Please give me a few minutes before I reorganise things. Would you both like to wait in the lounge, please? The refreshments will be on us."

"Thank you," said Aaradhya, her heart pumping rapidly in her chest. She was going to spend some more time with this hunk, who had slept throughout the journey from Amsterdam to Delhi, waking up but a few minutes before landing. That too, only because the air hostess had woken him up.

"That would be great. I could do with a decent cup of coffee," he said to the crew member before turning to look at Aaradhya, "Shall we go? By the way, I am

Advik." A corner of his shapely mouth lifted in a half smile as he gave her his hand.

A mesmerised Aaradhya placed her hand in his large one, giving him a small smile of her own. "You slept through the whole flight," she said, half accusingly, "You were tired, I suppose."

"Beat, actually!" Shifting her hand to his left one, he pulled her along with him to the private lounge. The crew member had already called the people at the lounge, it seemed. They were treated like VIPs as they were shown to a comfortable sofa. "A cappuccino for me, please. And you? What's your name?"

If there was any hint of curiosity in his dark gaze, she couldn't see it. "I am Aaradhya. You can call me Aara." Turning to the waiter, she said, "I'll have a latte, please."

"Anything to eat, sir, madam?" asked the waiter.

"I'll have an *aloo paratha,*" said Advik.

"Nothing for me."

After the waiter left, Advik asked, an eyebrow up in query, "Sure?"

She smiled, her brown eyes lighting up. "I had a huge dinner. And have not had an opportunity to exercise."

"Oh yeah, I missed dinner."

Her smile stretched into a lazy grin, her heart beat pacing out as she slowly relaxed. "That's right."

Grimacing, he gave a nod, his attention back on his phone.

Aaradhya wasn't one to give up so easily. "Do you live in Mumbai? Or are you visiting the city?"

"I was born and brought up in Mumbai."

She gave a happy nod. "Same here." She tried asking him a few more things like his school and college background only to receive monosyllables in reply. Just when she gave up her effort at conversation, the waiter returned with their orders.

Ravenous, Advik attacked his *paratha,* ignoring her completely. She avidly watched him munch his way through the many slices, pausing to sip from his water glass from time to time. She found it so incredible that he didn't want to chat. It was truly a first experience for her, to be side-lined by a handsome guy who seemed more interested in the food on his plate than the beautiful woman sitting across from him.

He suddenly looked up to find her staring at him. Appearing sheepish, he pushed his half-full plate towards her. "Would you like some?"

She picked one slice and pushed the plate right back at him, muttering, "Thanks," and watched him gobbling the rest of it even before she managed to finish eating the one slice.

The Indigo crew member came to the lounge looking for them. "Ahem! Sir, madam. A small hiccup," he said, looking at them warily.

"What happened?" asked Aaradhya, noticing Advik's full mouth.

"There are no flights to Mumbai today. We can accommodate you in the afternoon flight tomorrow." He lifted a hand when Advik would have spoken. "I apologise for the inconvenience. Please forgive me. But I'll ensure that you have a proper accommodation for tonight. We have booked rooms for you at The Park. A vehicle will take you there. I once again apologise for the trouble caused."

Advik looked at Aaradhya for a moment before turning to the other man. "What cannot be cured and all that. It's alright, buddy." He turned to his cup of coffee and sat back to relish it as if he had no care in the world.

She had been so eagerly waiting to get back to her family. Tch! But then, just as he had said, 'what could not be cured had to be endured'. Aaradhya shrugged, responding to the airline crew member, "Okay, I suppose. Actually, I am ready to go to my room now." She turned to lift an eyebrow at Advik.

"Me too," he agreed, getting up from his chair.

Advik offered to push the trolley that held their three suitcases while Aaradhya dragged her trolley bag as they followed the airline crew member to the exit. He waved to a driver and soon, a Maruti Ertiga came and stood in front of them. Between the driver and the crew member, they loaded all the luggage in the boot before Aaradhya and Advik settled in the back seat.

Aaradhya, who had been too excited to sleep on the flight, went to her room to crash on her bed, not waking up till dinner time; that too only when her room phone rang. "Hello." Her voice came out in a dry croak.

"Hello, Ms Aaradhya. I am calling from the hotel reception. I am calling because Mr Advik had left instructions to wake you up at eight pm. He…"

"Huh! What time is it?" she asked. Surely, it couldn't be eight, not already. She had gone to sleep before noon.

"It's eight o' clock, ma'am. That's why I am calling. Sorry if I disturbed you. But…"

"No, no, that's okay. Did Advik leave any other message for me?" she asked, getting up to sit on the bed.

"Mr Advik said he will be at Agni, the bar and lounge. It would be nice if you could join him."

"Oh, alright. Fine, thanks for the message." Aaradhya disconnected the call. The man was weird. Couldn't he have called her himself? Instead of leaving it to the receptionist?

Well, she mentally shrugged, *people were different, weren't they?*

Sliding out of the bed, she walked into the bathroom. Aaradhya didn't spend time checking out the luxurious appointments as she set the water to the right temperature before having a shower. She was famished after that single slice of paratha for breakfast. Drying herself, she pulled on a strapless bra and matching panties in cream lace before wearing a strapless peach coloured jersey dress that had gathered no creases from all the travelling. It faithfully followed the shape of her upper body till her slim waist before flaring into a short skirt that fell a couple of inches above her knees. She clipped on a pair of matching drop earrings which touched her bare shoulders before stepping into peach-coloured pumps of a darker shade.

Aaradhya dusted a light coat of powder on her face and neck before applying mascara to her lashes and a soft peach gloss to her lush lips. Stepping back, she ran her fingers through her straight hair, fluffing it up to add volume before turning left and right to check herself out. Five feet and seven inches tall with a slim figure—though she was personally thrilled with her plump breasts—Aaradhya was an attractive woman.

Placing her lip gloss and room keys along with a packet of wet wipes in a cream and gold clutch, she left her room to take the elevator down to Agni.

Advik had turned around in his barstool to sit facing the entrance to the lounge. He lifted a hand when he saw his co-passenger walking into the bar.

As she wound her way between the dancers who thronged the wooden floor, Aaradhya had eyes only for the handsome man who had been her so silent travelling companion from Amsterdam to Delhi and was to continue to travel with her to Mumbai the next day. If possible, he looked handsomer than before. He wore a pastel blue linen jacket over a collarless white shirt paired with dark blue designer jeans. His feet were encased in dark brown leather moccasins. Lifting her gaze to his face as she got closer, she noticed that his long hair was brushed back neatly and fell all the way down to his shoulders. The handlebar moustache was a perfect frame to his manly lips, the lower one only a shade thicker than the thin upper one. His nose was sharp and slightly hooked at the tip; his forehead broad. His deep black eyes were widely placed, framed by naturally thick and well-shaped eyebrows.

Aaradhya stopped in her tracks, hastily bringing her gaze down to the floor when she realised that she was standing too close to him. So close, that she could see her own reflection in his eyes.

Getting down from his stool, Advik drew the one next to his and gestured for her to sit down.

Chivalrous! Aaradhya's gaze went wide with surprise as she climbed on to the stool. "Thanks!"

After climbing back into his seat, he asked, "What would you like to drink?" turning to lift a finger to beckon the bartender.

"Gin and lemon with lots of ice. Oh, and something to munch. I'm famished."

He gave her a half smile. "I guess. They have a choice of finger foods." He opened the menu and pushed it towards her. "Any preferences?" he asked, placing orders for their drinks; a gin cocktail for her and a whiskey and soda for himself with lots of ice.

"I love all kinds of food, though vegetarian," she said, running her gaze down the menu before placing her finger at the top. "Lebanese veg platter. Do you mind sharing? It's too much food for one person." She hesitated before continuing, "Unless you'd prefer something else."

He shrugged. "Works for me," he responded succinctly before placing the order for the food with the waiter who walked up to them.

"Are you visiting home before returning to the USA?" she asked.

"Back home for good," he replied briefly, drinking deeply from his glass.

She took a few sips of her cocktail, feeling restless. Turning to look at the DJ who was belting out some Bollywood tunes, she asked, "Do you want to dance?"

Advik gave her a startled glance as if he couldn't really fathom the meaning of her words.

A sudden feeling of irritation engulfing her, Aaradhya jumped off her stool to move to the middle of the floor where a number of people were already swinging to the music the DJ had put on. She joined them, dancing her way through a few numbers before she noticed that Advik had joined her on the floor as well. They didn't talk as they swung to the music, dancing around each other without touching.

By now, only too aware that he was not interested in talking, Aaradhya stuck to monosyllables as they munched on the pitta bread and hummus along with the olives and stuffed peppers. *Yummy!* She told herself, not keen to begin another conversation with Advik. Maybe he was the moody type. Anyway, they were here together just for today. And may not even cross each other's paths once they reached Mumbai.

Aaradhya got down from the barstool after finishing her meal and just the one drink. Pretending to yawn, she said, "I think I'll call it a night." She didn't bother to ask if they could travel together to the airport the next day. What did it matter? Okay, he was an attractive hunk! So what?! It didn't seem as if he wanted to know her more. Mentally shrugging her slender shoulders, she took the elevator to her room, calling her best friend to chat with her late into the night.

Shaking her head to come out of her reminiscences, Aaradhya stepped out of the swimming pool to towel herself dry...

Though she had travelled to Delhi airport by the same car as Advik; on the flight, they had taken seats on opposite sides of the aisle and had not spoken to each other after that, going their separate ways.

Tch! Why the hell am I thinking of the man? I know nothing about him other than the fact that he's extremely handsome and suave. Okay, he was chivalrous too! She didn't even know his full name, let alone where he lived in Mumbai.

In another part of Mumbai, at the same witching hour in Bandra, Advik paced the living room of his small apartment that wasn't far from the family home which was a few buildings away.

Aware of his grandfather Bhaskar Hegde's stubborn nature—well, he had inherited the same attitude, hadn't he—Advik had rented a separate apartment. After all, hadn't he been categorically told that he wasn't welcome back in his family home? It was his own father who had brought the message from his grandfather.

If Advik had tried a little harder, persuading his grandmother Akshatha to side with him, he could have easily returned to his room on the top floor of the duplex. But there was a reason why Advik had refrained from doing so. After all the effort he had put in to study in New York and work with a number of restaurants in both the USA and Europe, he didn't see the sense in returning to the Hegde stranglehold. Yes, that's what it was, a stranglehold, the reins held solely by his grandfather, Bhaskar Hegde. When he said 'jump', that's exactly what all his family members did. That is, except for Advik. And that was exactly the reason why he hadn't bothered to fight his grandfather's decision to keep Advik away from home.

It had been almost a week since his return to Mumbai, but he still couldn't forget the woman he had met on the flight from Amsterdam to Delhi and again from Delhi to Mumbai.

Aaradhya!

He couldn't deny the fact that she was too damn beautiful. But just now, he did not have the time for a girlfriend. He had had his quota of fun, having had three affairs with fun-loving young women, all foreigners, in foreign lands. After all, he had been clear that he wanted no complications but only fun partners in bed. And he had got exactly that!

Even before travelling back to India, Advik had promised himself that he was going to concentrate completely on building his career. After all, he had to prove himself a success in the restaurant business, not just for his own sake, but for his grandfather's. The stubborn old man thought only he knew best. And it was up to Advik to prove otherwise. While he loved his grandfather, Advik was completely aware of the octogenarian's faults.

What Advik had not expected was to feel a sharp kick to his solar plexus when his gaze fell on the woman sitting right next to him on the flight from Amsterdam. He had done his best to keep his distance from her, even trying to go to sleep the minute the flight took off. While he had shut his eyes firmly, he had been too conscious of her sitting next to him. It had been a long time and a number of deep breaths before sleep had claimed him.

But look at what had happened when they were trying to catch the connecting flight to Mumbai. He wondered if it was fate that had been at play there. Doing his best to keep his attention from going to her, he had glued himself to his phone as he stood in the queue at the check-in counter at Delhi airport, not aware that she was standing ahead of him.

When the airline crew member wanted two people to give up their seats, he had immediately volunteered, without being aware that the other volunteer was Aaradhya. He had been in no hurry to return and face his grandfather back home. Which was the reason why he had been ready to postpone his return without having to think twice.

Advik didn't quite know why his mood had suddenly plummeted. Home had been a happy place once upon a time, when he had been a child who was unaware of the power politics played by his grandfather, Bhaskar Hegde. His life had been fun before he got to know the reason for his uncle Kartik's bachelor state. His grandfather may be a brilliant chef and an even better restaurateur. But he was a horrible head of the Hegde family. Or that's what Advik felt.

Grandfather and grandson had been at loggerheads before Advik left for his studies abroad…

Being the only grandchild of Bhaskar Hegde, owner and chef of Mysuru Ahara, brought with it, its own pressure. While Advik had loved to cook even as a kid—he used to tag along with his grandfather every evening after school—he had always felt that there was more to restaurant food than what was being served at the family restaurant. Yes, the restaurant was extremely popular and gave a good deal of competition to Madras Meals, the parent company. But that was not enough, not for Advik. He knew that his grandfather, his father Ganesh and his uncle Kartik, were extremely happy with what they had.

But Advik had grown up watching Masterchef shows. He knew there was a whole world out there that had passed them by. He wanted to be a part of that world. That's when he had decided to enrol himself in the Institute of Culinary Education, New York.

War had ensued in the Hegde household when Advik had announced his decision almost six years ago.

"What nonsense is this, Advik?" his grandfather had yelled, before he turned to glare at Ganesh. "You must have known that your son was going to do this. Didn't you advise him against it? It's ridiculous throwing hard-earned money to learn something that we already know. Cooking is in our blood. Cancel your admission, Advik, NOW."

Advik leaned back against a marble pillar, his stance chilled, unperturbed as he watched his grandfather who appeared to be on the verge of bursting a vein. The old man still had a stranglehold on the business and kept a tight rein on the family finances.

Advik also turned his head to look at his father, feeling sorry for him. But he was made of sterner stuff. He wasn't one to be curbed by anyone else. So what if the family finances didn't provide enough? He had earned one legacy from his grandfather—that of hard work. He had begun to do odd jobs even when he was barely sixteen and had saved all his earnings. When he had finished college, it was expected of Advik to work at the family restaurant, Mysuru Ahara. He did that, but for exactly eight hours in a day. No amount of scolding from his grandfather or father could stop Advik from taking off the moment his eight hours were done.

Over and above that, Advik had insisted on taking a salary for his work, equal to any restaurant manager. Kartik adored his nephew and was thrilled that here was someone who could not be browbeaten by Bhaskar Hegde. And Advik also knew how to wind his grandmother Akshatha around his little finger. The arrogant and snooty matriarch danced to her only grandchild's tunes.

And thus, at twenty-three, Advik had saved a lot of money, having invested it intelligently. He had more than enough to give himself a culinary education in the USA—both culinary arts as well as pastry and baking. He planned to complete both courses in the span of sixteen months and work his way around the USA and maybe Europe.

None of Bhaskar's tantrums and scolding had an effect on Advik, who went about preparing for his trip. When his father Ganesh tried to reason with his son, Advik hugged the older man and said, "Dad, the world is changing and we need to change along with it, unless we want to be left behind. Bhaskar *Ajja* is old-fashioned. I know he's built an excellent restaurant with great food and even better business prospects. But tell me something, Dad, how much have we grown in the past couple of decades? We are serving the same food. I realise that maintaining quality is a wonderful thing. But people nowadays want more variety, and something new, all the time. Isn't it part of our heritage as restaurateurs to cater to the need of customers?"

Ganesh gave his son a stunned look even as Kartik clapped loudly, walking into his nephew's room where the father-son duo had been chatting. He hugged his nephew and said, "I'm so proud of you, Advik. You are absolutely right. We need to grow with the world. I did try telling the old dinosaur that. But then, you know…"

"Kartik, mind your tongue. You can't speak about *Appa* like that." Ganesh reprimanded his younger brother as he had no answer to his son's questions.

"Says who?" asked Kartik in a bitter voice. "That's the only freedom I have, that of speaking my mind.

Are you saying that I might lose that also in the immediate future?"

Ganesh shook his head. "Stop it, Kartik. Here I am, trying to dissuade Advik from making a mistake. He's going to waste a lot of money in going to America and learn what we already know…"

Kartik burst out laughing. "Pull you head out of the soil where it's buried, Ganesh. Advik is going to the US to learn what we don't know. And it will do us all good," he declared vehemently, patting his nephew's shoulder.

Advik looked from his father to his uncle and back again, not uttering a word.

"You don't get it, Kartik. *Appa* won't let Advik join us in running Mysuru Ahara if he doesn't listen to him. How will he survive? I'm worried about that." There was a heavy frown on Ganesh's face as he glared at his younger brother. "Isn't it enough that you have spoilt your life by remaining a bachelor just because you won't listen to *Appa*? Why do you want to spoil Advik's life also now?"

"That's unfair, Dad. And you know it. It wasn't Kartik *Chitthaiya's* fault that he's a bachelor. He's one because of *Ajja* and *Ajji* and their stubborn attitude. And how can he spoil my life, Dad? Going to the USA is my choice and no one else's." Advik voiced his protest without raising his voice. "And as for *Ajja* not letting me back into the family business, there's no need to worry so much about it. If I have to set up my own restaurant, I most definitely will. After all, if

Bhaskar *Ajja* could do it in 1960, I can definitely do it fifty-eight years later, in 2018. I…"

"How long do you plan to be abroad?" asked Ganesh, his mouth opening wide in astonishment. It was only 2013 now.

Advik shrugged. "The courses I am planning to take should get done in a year and a half or maybe less. I plan to work in restaurants in America and Europe. So, maybe three years or at the most, four."

Ganesh grimaced, realising that his son's plans were set. And Advik could be as stubborn as his grandfather. He felt as if he was caught between the devil and the deep blue sea. "Does your mother know of your plans?" Vrunda's life revolved around her son. What if her heart broke when she got to know that he was going to live on the other side of the world over the next few years?

"Of course, Dad. I've been discussing this with Mom from the beginning." He had been talking about it with his uncle too and had made Kartik promise that he wouldn't let out the plan until everything was in place. It wasn't as if Ganesh was learning about it for the first time. Only, he had never taken his son seriously whenever Advik mentioned going to America for further studies.

"And she doesn't mind?"

"Mind what, Dad? I'm going for higher education. Why would she mind?"

Ganesh shook his head, a sad expression on his face. He didn't much care for his life playing second fiddle to his father. He could understand that his son wasn't keen either. In a way he was glad that Advik had decided to carve his own path. It was probably for the best. That his father was a control freak was something he couldn't deny.

He nodded now, placing a hand on Advik's broad shoulder. "I wish you luck, my son. My blessings are with you. I'm sure you will do very well. Will you keep in touch?"

"Dad!" Advik hugged his father, pulling his uncle also into the circle. "Of course, I will. I'll just be a phone call away. And when I set up my own restaurant, Kartik uncle will be going into partnership with me, okay?"

Both the older men gave Advik startled looks, shock on Ganesh's face and joy on Kartik's.

"You must be the best nephew in the world, Advik," said Kartik, hugging him close. "I'll hold you to that promise."

Ganesh shook his head at both of them, only too aware that things had never been in his control, ever.

Advik came back to the present, a soft, inadvertent smile on his face as his mind went back to Aaradhya all at once…

After giving up his flight ticket, he had been thrown together with Aaradhya for a whole day and night. That is, fate had tried its hand to do just that! But luckily, she had been totally jet-lagged and had gone to sleep for the whole day. While he had wandered the streets of Delhi aimlessly, suddenly able to understand what Devdas must have undergone after losing the love of his life.

Huh!

He had to strongly curb his instincts to call her room. Instead, he had left instructions with the receptionist to wake Aaradhya up for dinner.

His heart had skipped several beats before thundering away in his chest when he saw her walk into Agni, the lounge bar. Oh my God! The short dress of a pinkish orange colour—he wasn't sure which shade it was actually, nor did he care—made her appear tall, her legs so slim and long, making his mouth water at the sight. Her lightly made-up face glowed in the twinkling lights of the bar, her eyes sparkling vivaciously. Her bare shoulders gleamed, making him curl his hands into fists. Otherwise, he wouldn't have been able to refrain from touching her soft skin that made him drool.

Innate chivalry made him get down from his barstool to help her on to the one next to his. After that, he had done his best to speak as less as possible, only too aware of her disappointment.

Well, what else was he to do? A girlfriend would need time and attention. And he didn't have either as he wanted to concentrate on his job and plan his own restaurant. He couldn't afford to hook up with a woman for at least the next two or three years.

But, damn it! Advik lifted a cushion off the sofa to throw it against the far wall with all his might. While his mind was clear about his plans, his heart refused to listen, it seemed.

No, no, no! He was not going to think of her. He had such a huge commitment to himself and to his family.

Falling back on the sofa, he switched on the TV to watch Brooklyn Nine-Nine on Netflix, his mind not actually in it. He didn't really care as he had watched the first five seasons already. He stared at the TV, completely tuned out of the heated argument between Jake Peralta and Amy Santiago; his mind right back to where it had been—on the lovely Aaradhya.

3

After packing away all the baked goodies to be sent to their restaurant, Madras Meals, Aaradhya untied her apron and picked up a cup of piping hot *masala chai* to go sit on the balcony. While she sipped from her cup, she ran through her social media handles on her phone, not really interested in either the WhatsApp messages, Facebook updates or Instagram pictures.

Tch!

How did one find a guy by just knowing his first name in a huge city like Mumbai? It was definitely like looking for a needle in a haystack. But a man in his twenties must definitely have social media accounts, right?

Cheering up immensely, Aaradhya opened her Facebook app to search for Advik from Mumbai. After scrawling through at least fifty profiles out of a few hundreds, she gave up with a sigh. Damn!

The result wasn't all that different on Instagram and Twitter as well. She didn't even bother with LinkedIn. After all, she had no clue as to what profession he was in, *presuming he had one to speak of,* she thought spitefully to herself.

It seemed rather abnormal for a single and handsome man to ignore a fairly beautiful woman such as herself. What could be wrong? Suddenly turning pale, Aaradhya wondered if she was mistaken in thinking that he was single.

Maybe he was already hitched!

Oh my God! Did that mean she was wasting her time hankering after a man who already had a girlfriend or maybe even a wife? How dumb was that?!

She quickly got up from the cane chair she had been sitting on and went to the kitchen to wash her tea cup before going to her room. Changing out of the shorts and t-shirt she had been wearing during her baking session, Aaradhya quickly wore a pair of slim fitting jeans and a sleeveless top in red. Sliding her feet into a pair of denim slip-on shoes, she left the apartment after calling out to her grandmother. She needed to get out of the house or she might go mad thinking about Advik, the man who was so obviously not interested in her. Grr!

She walked over to Madras Meals and got in everyone's way as the place was run to overflowing with evening customers who had stepped in for coffee and snacks. Smiling when she noticed the demand for the pastries that had been introduced on the menu, she walked over to the accounts counter where her grandfather Ramani was seated.

"Thatha!"

Ramani looked up from the cash register to see his favourite grandchild standing in front of him. With a wide smile of greeting, he said, "Aaradhya! So glad to see you, my child. Did you notice the cake counter? It's almost half empty."

Aaradhya grinned back at her grandfather, her irritation disappearing for the moment. "Yes, *Thatha,* I did. Isn't that amazing?"

He shook his head, his eyes twinkling. "Not so amazing if you consider the fact that they taste so delicious. The pricing is so reasonable too."

She gave him a happy nod. "I'm glad I came here, *Thatha*."

"Something has been troubling you even before you returned home from Europe." He didn't frame the words as a question, but more like a declaration.

Aaradhya's lips drooped at the corners. "You're right as always, *Thatha*. You are too wise, I suppose."

"Do you want to talk about it? I can slip away from here for a short while and we can have some coffee, if you want," he offered.

Aaradhya knew for a fact that Ramani didn't care to drink coffee after four in the afternoon as it kept him awake late into the night. He was only trying to make an extra effort on her behalf. And anyway, she was not really ready to share her feeling of disturbance with anyone. After all, what could she say? That she was attracted to a stranger who didn't want to meet her again? That she knew nothing about him other than his first name?

Tch!

Shaking her head, she said, "I was just passing by, *Thatha*. And stopped to say 'hello'. You carry on. I can see that you are really busy." He had rung up four bills during the few minutes she had stood at the counter in front of him. "I will get on with my walk, okay? We'll catch up during dinner."

"Alright. I'll see you, my child." Ramani turned his attention to the hovering waiter who wanted yet another bill made.

Aaradhya stepped out of the busy restaurant not all that far from Matunga East railway station and walked along the busy thoroughfare before turning into a quiet by lane. Her eyes automatically fell on Mysuru Ahara which took up the corner plot on the left side. The restaurant belonged to the Hegdes. She recalled the hair-raising tales she had heard about how her grandfather Ramani Iyer and the owner of Mysuru Ahara, Bhaskar Hegde, had arrived in Bombay on the same day. Both the young men had been interested in cooking and setting up a restaurant business in Bombay. Ramani and Bhaskar had done just that, working hard to make their common dream come true. And that's how Madras Meals had been born.

But later, there had been a fallout; and the owners of the restaurant had split up, resulting in one more place called Mysuru Ahara. Aaradhya wasn't too clear about the details. But she knew that her aunt, Janani, was a spinster only because she couldn't marry the man she loved, someone who belonged to the Hegde family. She had heard whispers, but no one had given her all the details. Nor had she asked many questions.

After all, it was an old story. And she wasn't keen to hurt Janani by bringing it up after all these years.

Matunga was big enough to hold both the restaurants with customers thronging the portals morning, noon and night.

She had gathered a few more bits and pieces over time. Her grandfather Ramani had a large heart and still loved his once-upon-a-time best friend, Bhaskar and held no bitter feelings towards the Hegde family despite his own daughter, Janani, insisting on remaining a spinster. Aaradhya had heard from different sources that Bhaskar himself—who had always been more serious than her own grandfather—had turned angry and bitter after the fallout. It was the sons who had borne the brunt of the old man's temper. She had also heard of an only grandson who had gone abroad.

Mentally shrugging, Aaradhya continued on her walk, glad that her grandfather was the cheerful man he was. How she adored him!

The moment she stepped into the quiet lane, Aaradhya's thoughts went back to Advik. A deep sigh shuddering through her body, she slipped into a jog, hoping to forget the dratted man, succeeding only partially even as her mind whirled around the different ways to find him.

Returning home, she had a quick shower before sitting with her phone, following an idea that had taken root in her mind during her walk. Downloading the Tinder App, she quickly opened an account before scrolling through the profiles of some men. Ugh! Each one was looking for a sleeping partner, even one-night stands. Grimacing, she quickly shut the app, throwing the phone down on her bed.

I hate you! She silently declared to herself, recalling Advik's handsome features. *I hate that you have so deeply rooted yourself in my mind that I am unable to forget you.* She quickly left her room to join her grandparents in the hall, deciding to spend the evening with them, confident that they would distract her from her disturbing thoughts.

It was way past midnight when Advik entered his apartment. It had been a really good day and he had enjoyed every moment of the time spent at his new job with Hot Foods. Though the plan was for him to learn all the ropes of the restaurant chain—they had eight different chains of restaurants serving a variety of cuisines from around the world—just now it seemed that he would play the role of trouble shooter. The job was challenging and took all his intelligence and skills to stay ahead.

After taking a shower, he pulled on a pair of boxers and sat back on the sofa, skimming through his phone. Seeing a number of Super Likes on his Tinder app, he opened it with a grimace. No, he wasn't at all keen on hooking up with any woman, especially those who lived halfway across the world. He quickly changed the location settings on his profile before looking through his own pictures. The main profile picture showed him wearing a brilliant white linen shirt, holding a balloon glass that was half-full of ruby red wine, his deep brown eyes crinkling at the corners as he grinned at whoever was clicking the camera. He couldn't quite remember who it had been, though he recalled the crazy all-night party where the picture had been shot. The rest of the pictures were of Advik playing basketball, showing off his washboard abs after flinging his t-shirt on the railing. It had been a hot day indeed. He was at least a foot up in the air, his brief shorts and blue sneakers the only bits of covering he had had on, his shoulder length hair held back by a scrunchy. It had the most likes, even more than the main profile picture that had a couple of thousand likes. He flipped through the rest of the pictures, shaking his head.

It was time to make some drastic changes. To begin with, he didn't really think the women who lived near his present location would be keen on brief love affairs. And just now, Advik wasn't interested in any kind of relationship, short or long ones. The best thing would be to upload a different set of pictures, more serious ones that showed him for what he was, a keen restaurateur. Deleting all the pictures except for the main one, Advik decided to change the pictures over the coming week.

As for Aaradhya, he didn't plan to spend his time thinking of her, not at all. Well, thoughts of the beautiful woman kept popping into his mind whenever he had a few free moments, but he had somehow managed to squash them to the back of his mind, every time. Though he couldn't deny that the effort was getting a bit harder with each subsequent attempt.

Tossing his phone on the adjacent sofa, he took the book he had been reading and opened it to the page where he had placed a bookmark and began to read. That he couldn't concentrate on Dan Brown's *Origin*—he had already read a third of the thriller before he stepped into the plane that had taken him to Amsterdam and had found it extremely interesting—irritated him no end. Shutting the book and keeping it aside, he jumped up from the sofa, walking up and down his living room.

Damn the woman! Why the hell does she have to get under my skin?!

4

"Didn't you say your guy's name was Advik?" asked Neeti, her eyes on her phone, her finger sliding over the images of a young and attractive man on Tinder, playing chef in a kitchen. "Do you think he believes that a way to a woman's heart; okay, maybe her bed, is through her stomach?" Neeti laughed, checking out the pictures. This Advik looked too damn attractive, with shoulder length hair, a handlebar moustache and laughing brown eyes. And damn sexy dimples on both cheeks, in all those pictures where he was laughing. All of which matched Aaradhya's description of him.

"What? Neeti, you aren't making sense. First of all, he's not my guy. And how would *you* know, when you have never set eyes on him? I have been through so many profiles on social media and have still not found him." Aaradhya's mouth drooped at the corners as she sipped from a tall glass of iced mochaccino. They were sitting at a coffee shop in Phoenix Market City, a huge shopping mall in Kurla.

"I think I have found him on Tinder," said Neeti Aggarwal, turning to wink at her best friend from school days.

"Meh!" Aaradhya ignored Neeti who was trying to push her phone under her nose.

"Check this profile," insisted Neeti.

"Huh!" Aaradhya turned away. "I checked on Tinder too. If I couldn't find him, how could you?"

"Why don't you have a look?" asked Neeti reasonably, reaching with her right hand to pick up her own iced latte. She was only taking a wild guess, trying to match Aaradhya's verbal description of the man she had met on her return flight home. It was all in fun.

"Tch!" With great reluctance, Aaradhya took her friend's phone in her hand. Another week had gone and she had stopped searching for Advik on social media. What was the use? Here she was, doing her best to forget the man and look at Neeti—supposedly her best friend—forcing her to remember him. Bringing her gaze to the screen, she looked at the man wearing a chef's cap, standing over a smoking skillet with a capsicum in one hand and a large knife in the other.

Whaaaaaaatttt!!!!!!!!!!

She shook her head as if to clear it before staring at the picture once again. It was Advik, definitely. Quickly scrolling through the pictures, her gaze went wide when she became a hundred per cent sure that it was the dratted man whom she had been searching for over two weeks.

'Advik 28,' said his Tinder profile. Executive Chef and Manager at Hot Foods! This time, she let her jaw drop, her mouth wide open as she stared disbelievingly at his profile. He was in the same profession as she was. Oh my God! Was this just a coincidence or the hand of providence?

"Neeti, I…" Aaradhya was speechless as she stared at her friend, a wide grin on her face. "It is him."

"Your Advik!" declared Neeti, a smug expression on her face.

Aaradhya couldn't help staring at Advik's picture. Pouting, she said, "He isn't mine, at least not yet." Quickly checking out his profile, she returned the phone to her friend before opening the Tinder app on her own. Finding Advik, she scrolled through his pictures once again, doing her best not to drool.

Truly it was an extra point in his favour that he was a chef. Now she wanted to get to know him more than ever. She swiped right on the Tinder app even as Neeti gasped.

"Are you sure, Aara?" asked Neeti in a stage whisper.

Aaradhya gave her friend a devilish grin. "Yep." She thought for a second before tapping the blue star icon in a Super Like, making Neeti gasp all the louder.

"Are you crazy, Aara?" asked Neeti, "You have been on Tinder for like how long? A little more than a week? You have not even swiped right once, let alone Super Like. Then how come…"

Aaradhya shrugged. "That's because I never came across any guy that I wanted to meet in person all this long."

"But you don't know much about him, except that he's an executive chef at Hot Foods, whatever that means. Have you heard of the company before?" Neeti was a tad anxious now. Social media was fun to meet new people. But there was also a lurking danger. What if it was someone with malicious intentions? From Aaradhya's behaviour, it was obvious that she was keen to connect with this Advik personally.

"Hot Foods? Yes, of course. It's a chain of restaurants serving different kinds of cuisines. We have been to their Chinese outlet. Remember?" Aaradhya quickly drew Neeti's attention to their Chinese lunch at Oberoi Mall in Malad three days back.

"Oh!" Neeti recalled that the food had been superb. Calming down some, she still said in a warning voice, "I think you should go slow. He..."

Too excited to heed her friend's warning, Aaradhya threw back her head and laughed. "You are joking. If I go any slower, the neighbourhood snail would get there before me. What's up with you, Neeti? It has been two whole weeks since I met Advik. You know very well I have been searching for him all over Facebook and Insta. It was a lucky chance that you found him today. Now that I know how to get in touch with him, what do you expect? That I sit back and wait for things to move forward? You think the man is going to jump in front of me and ask me for a candlelight dinner?" Her voice was bitter with sarcasm. It was only too obvious to Aaradhya that Advik had felt no spark of interest in her. But that didn't mean she couldn't make it happen. At least, she planned to try. It was not like her to sit back and wait for things to happen to her. She had liked Advik on sight and she wanted to know him more. Gone were the days when it was the guy who had to make the first move.

I am from the new millennium and I plan to make full use of it, declared Aaradhya to herself.

Neeti gave her friend a tentative smile, able to understand her impatience. Aaradhya had always been a go-getter, even from their school days. She worked hard and was keen to give her best to every project she got involved in, personal or professional. Just now, she was keen to date Advik, nothing more, but then nothing less either. She only hoped that Advik was a decent guy for Aaradhya's sake. With a small sigh of capitulation, Neeti said, "I suppose you're right. I…"

Aaradhya slapped the table with her right hand, making the empty glasses rattle. "I know I am. Just you wait and watch me go on at least one date with Advik."

Feeling rather sorry for Advik by now, Neeti gave Aaradhya a small smile and a thumbs up. "I'm sure you will do it."

"After seeing these pics, I've a good mind to add food pictures to my profile too." Continuing with her own line of thought, Aaradhya spoke in a soft voice. She was a foodie through and through. After all, she had spent almost two years in Switzerland doing a couple of courses at the reputed Culinary Arts Academy as well as interning in four different hotels to gain experience in their five-star kitchens.

Aaradhya carried her grandfather Ramani Iyer's genes as well as her father Kumar Iyer's—Ramani's younger son—and cooking had been a passion from the time when she was a child. While her father and her Uncle Chandar—Ramani's eldest born—had been happy to learn the skills from their own father, Aaradhya had been keen to spread her wings. She wanted to bring international cuisine into their kitchen at Madras Meals.

When she had first thought of it, she had run the idea by her grandfather, since she always went to him for advice.

"But, little one, world cuisine means that you might have to include non-veg dishes into our menu. And I don't think…"

"No, no, *Thatha*." Aaradhya had been quick to reassure her grandfather as she hugged him. "That's not necessarily true. So many people around the world are turning into vegetarians and some have even taken a further step and become vegans. I plan to learn the different flavours, blends and masalas from this academy. After that, I will combine it with our dishes and create our own signature style. Don't you think that's a good idea?" She looked up at Ramani's face, her black eyes glowing with enthusiasm and mischief.

Ramani gave his granddaughter a proud look. Aaradhya was definitely smart and was as enthusiastic as he had been at her age. And over time, his love for creating food had only increased instead of diminishing. Once his sons had grown up, Ramani had given the business reins over to them and taken over the kitchen, playing head chef. The past twenty or so years had been the happiest in his life. An inadvertent sigh rushed to the surface when he recalled his first journey from Madras to Bombay, meeting Bhaskar Hegde at VT Station.

Things had changed so drastically since those days and so dramatically too. Some changes for the good and the others not so good. One bad thing had been the loss of his friend and partner; not to death, but to something even worse: enmity.

He pulled his mind back to the present when he heard Aaradhya speak again. "You haven't answered me, *Thatha*," she grumbled, shaking his arm.

Ramani smiled down at her. "You are right, Aara, as always. Your idea is not just good, my child. It's brilliant!" he declared. "You must go and do this course. I can't wait to taste what you will be bringing to our table. I wonder if it's time to give Madras Meals a complete rehaul?!" he asked, lifting a heavy salt and pepper brow at her in query.

Aaradhya gurgled with laughter as she moved away from him to twirl around in a dance like movement, too excited to contain herself. "Not yet, *Thatha*. I'll call you from Geneva once I am finished with the culinary course. I want to also learn to make pastry and chocolate at Lucerne. That and my internship will take a few months. You can have the rehaul done during that period. What say?"

"Smart girl." Ramani nodded. Of all his three grandchildren, it was Aaradhya who was keen to carry on the family legacy. Chandar's sons Abhishek and Raghav were both in the IT industry, one based in the USA and the other in the UK. That was the reason why Ramani had a special soft corner for his granddaughter. "We have a deal. You go and finish your course and call me from Geneva."

"Thank you, *Thatha*. You're the best." Aaradhya hugged her grandfather once again, throwing her arms around his neck. "I love you, so so much."

Ramani placed his hand on her head, blessing her with all his heart.

Dragging her thoughts back to the present, Aaradhya looked at Neeti who was sitting across from her, continuing to look into her phone…

"Hey, what are you checking now?" she asked Neeti.

"Huh!" Neeti lifted a dazed face to Aaradhya, having forgotten where she was and with whom. "Er… I…"

Aaradhya reached across to grab her friend's phone to see what she had been looking at before bursting out laughing. Neeti had been watching cat videos on Instagram.

"What's so funny?" asked Neeti, glaring at the other woman.

Aaradhya shrugged. "I was laughing at the cat's antics," she said, without batting an eyelid. "Really funny."

"If you say so," pouted Neeti, taking her phone back.

5

Advik Hegde smiled in amusement when he saw the Super Like on his profile. He had never thought that his food pictures would draw much attention on Tinder. He had opened an account on the hook-up app, hoping to get a girlfriend during his lonely days in New York. His course had been hectic, at least the way he had crammed extra hours into his schedule, to learn as much as possible in the least possible time. And the app had been helpful in finding him a partner in bed. It had taken him some time to find out what actually worked. He had checked a number of profiles in the top category and had realised that the best way to rise to the top was to post really great pictures. He had made the effort and it had worked really well for him. While he got more than a couple of thousand likes and even a number of Super Likes, he had matched up with only three girls over the few years he had been abroad. They had been open to a short-term relationship with him. It had worked well for them as well as him.

But back in India and with his location set to Mumbai, he wanted to keep a low profile on Tinder and had gone about it with the same determination like before. He had posted pictures of himself as the Chef he was, toning down the raw masculinity which he used to project before. He had been confident that women would stop chasing him now. And how much ever he wanted to keep away from relationships, he was not keen to let go of the Tinder account he had worked on for so long and hard.

He had been glad—at least that's what he had believed—when he hadn't received a single right swipe, let alone a Super Like, after returning to Mumbai. It was as if he was non-existent.

But today, he had got not just a right swipe but a click on the blue star too. Quickly opening the woman's profile, his eyes went wide when he saw who it was.

Aaradhya 23

He stared at the beautiful face of the young woman he had met on the KLM flight from Amsterdam, his heart thudding a tad too heavily within his chest. The very woman he had been trying to forget without any success.

Just now Advik looked at the main profile picture of Aaradhya on Tinder. She looked cute, with huge, dark eyes in an oval face ending in a pointed chin, her luscious pink lips bare of lipstick. It was framed by thick and straight long hair of a deep chestnut colour falling below her slender shoulders. He quickly ran his eyes over her profile before snapping his fingers. She was a chef too, trained in Switzerland.

Which meant that she was in the same profession as he was! It was simply too good to be true!

But... but... Advik grimaced. *I don't want any distraction, not at this point in my life. I have a career to build and speedily too.*

He opened the chat box in morbid fascination. What was the harm in saying 'hello'? After all, they had known each other for a day and a half, even if they had spent most of the hours sleeping—okay, separately. But they kind of knew each other, right?

Taking a deep and steadying breath, he typed into the chat box.

Hi Aara, how are you doing?

He waited for her to respond and was disappointed when there was no reply forthcoming. Shrugging mentally, Advik shut his phone and tucked it into his jeans' pocket before going about his work. Working as a manager with Hot Foods, he was learning the ropes of the business even as he planned to set up his own restaurant. Each time a chef at one of the multi-cuisine chain's restaurants wanted a day off, Advik stepped in, trying his hand at the huge variety that the restaurants had on offer—from Chinese to Thai to Japanese, Lebanese to Italian, Rajasthani to Gujarati, South Indian to Maharashtrian. He could manage to cook up a storm in every type of cuisine—non-vegetarian, vegetarian, vegan; you name it and he could make it—even coming up with special fusions of his own, wowing the customers as well as the owners of Hot Foods.

It was past midnight on Sunday—more than twenty-four hours later—when he received an update on his Tinder app. He opened his phone to see Aaradhya's reply. With a smile on his face, Advik placed his beer bottle on the table next to his sofa to check what she had to say.

Hi Advik, I'm good. Sorry for the late reply. Got time just now. How are you?

No problem. I'm all good. I see that you are a chef too. What do you cook?

A storm, no less

Advik smiled at her cheeky response. Her words were followed by a laughter emoticon, before she continued to chat.

And you?

Some with thunder and lightning too

Advik grinned to himself as he pressed the send button on that.

Hehe

The phone remained silent after that as if both were deep in thought. Realising that there wasn't anything more forthcoming from her end, he typed *bye* into the chat box before shutting the Tinder app. *No, I am not going to wait for her reply,* Advik promised to himself before shutting his phone.

Picking up his beer, he took a sip and grimaced when he perceived that it had gone flat. Pouring the contents down the kitchen sink, he took another bottle from the fridge before settling down in front of the TV.

One thing he had to appreciate about the woman. She had somehow managed to find him on Tinder, without even knowing his surname or his profession or anything at all expect his first name. Advik smiled to himself. Aaradhya was not just smart, she was also interested in cooking, in the restaurant business.

Should he take it as a sign from the universe? Advik shook his head to himself. NO DISTRACTIONS! Especially of the feminine kind. Not for the next couple of years, or at least until the time he set up his own restaurant.

He had enough trouble with a disapproving family. His grandfather, Bhaskar Hegde, had refused to speak to him after he returned from the USA. He hadn't approved of Advik going to study about something which came naturally to all the members of the Hegde family. But that had been almost six years ago. Advik had been confident that the old man would have forgiven him; probably because he must have missed his favourite grandchild. Only grandchild, actually.

Bhaskar Hegde had two sons—Ganesh and Kartik. Ganesh had married Vrunda and they had just the one son—Advik. Kartik Hegde had fallen in love with a woman, Bhaskar's partner's daughter, who belonged to the Tam Bram community. Bhaskar and his wife, Akshatha, had been against the match. Heartbroken, Kartik had decided to remain a bachelor. No amount of persuasion or threat could change his mind.

That left just Advik in the third generation of Hegdes. His grandfather had personally taught Advik how to create delicious food. In fact, Advik had spent all his free time in Mysuru Ahara's kitchen; sometimes even the kitchen at home. He had loved every moment of it, learning to make a whole range of food items, from starters to main courses to desserts. Everything was from South India, though, especially Karnataka, the state Bhaskar hailed from.

Belonging to the new millennium, Advik had taken to visiting every kind of restaurant in Mumbai; whether street carts or five-star, it did not matter to him, as long as they served delicious fare. He had explored and experimented, falling in love with all kinds of food from around the world. It was this passion that had brought forth the idea of going abroad to study world cuisine. He had also mapped out those few years of both studying at a popular culinary school and gaining hands-on experience with world-renowned restaurants across the USA and Europe. Which is exactly what he had been doing over the past few years before returning home to Mumbai.

But this was precisely something that did not sit well with his grandfather, making Bhaskar so angry with his grandson that he had stopped speaking to Advik. While doing his best to keep his chin and morale up, Advik was hurt, deeply.

He had been at Agni, the lounge bar in Delhi, having a drink when his father, Ganesh, had called him…

"Hello, Dad," Advik greeted his father enthusiastically, a wide smile on his face. "I can't wait to get home, Dad. It's been a long five years, actually."

"Hello, Advik." Ganesh's voice was a little too quiet, totally lacking in enthusiasm, making Advik sit up and take note.

"Is everything alright, Dad?" he asked, his grip on his phone tightening as sudden anxiety ran through his nerves.

"Yes, yes. Everything's fine, son. I…"

Duh! It couldn't be more obvious that his father was stuck for words. Ganesh wasn't one given to hemming and hawing his way through a conversation, especially not with his own son.

"Dad! Tell me what's wrong? Is it *Ajja*? Is he ill?"

Ganesh gave a humourless laugh. "Your grandfather is hale and hearty." He was rather sarcastic when he made the statement, as if he almost wished that Bhaskar wasn't as healthy as a horse. "It's just that…"

Advik sighed, catching on. "He's still angry with me," he declared before taking a big gulp of his whisky and soda. Bhaskar had refused to take his call, had never spoken to him whenever he called home. Each time he had a valid excuse, or so Advik had convinced himself. But he could see it all clearly now. His grandfather had not forgiven Advik for planning his own life; his future.

Ganesh sighed. "That's right. He… I… Listen, Advik, I have booked you a room at Hotel Ashray International in Sion, which is not far from Matunga. Your mother and I will meet you there. When is your flight landing, did you say?"

Advik's mouth fell open. *Am I hearing right?* "Are you saying that you don't want me to come home?" he asked, his voice a hoarse whisper. Unable to believe his ears, he wanted his father to reiterate his words. *Maybe I would understand better if I heard it the second time.*

Ganesh groaned. "It's not me, Advik. If I had it in my right, I want you home, by my side. But no! It's always about your grandfather," he said bitterly. "It's always what he wants; what he commands. I should have listened to Kartik," he ranted, "The old man has a stranglehold on all of us, holding all the money. Do you realise that your father doesn't have more than a few thousand rupees to spend every month? Anything I want or need, more than that, I have to beg from my father. Wait on his benevolence…"

"…which is pretty non-existent." Advik completed his father's sentence, an angry smile on his face. "Do you understand why I insisted on receiving a salary when I worked at Mysuru Ahara? I always knew this, Dad. I don't quite understand how you could have missed something that was happening right under your nose. Look at Kartik *Chitthaiya's* state! He's going through hell. And all because of Bhaskar *Ajja*. I don't know why you both put up with his nonsense. Fuck the old man!" Advik was vehement as he cursed his grandfather. The strange thing was that he loved the old man too, despite all his faults.

"Advik! How could you speak like that?" Ganesh was shocked to hear his son swear so forcefully against the grandfather he adored.

"I can, Dad! And I will too. You can't deny that *Ajja* is trying to fuck up all our lives. He has already done it to you and *Chitthaiya*. But not mine, okay? I'll never let him do it to me," he swore, his voice soft, but intense.

Ganesh felt torn between anguish and a sense of pride in his son. "I truly appreciate the fact that you have somehow managed to strike your own path.

Despite being so young, you are truly wise, my son. I…" His voice gave out as emotion overtook him.

"Dad! Don't be upset. Everything happens for a reason. And *Ajja* is not completely bad. After all, he has given us a legacy; such a great restaurant which is so well known all over the city. I will reach Mumbai in the evening. I will call you on my way to Hotel Ashray International."

"The hotel isn't all that far from Sion station. You…"

"I know the location, Dad. No worries. Will you bring Mom with you?"

"As if she's going to let me meet you all by myself." Ganesh gave a relieved laugh. He had literally been biting his nails from the time his father had told him clearly that Advik wasn't welcome back at home.

Father and son chatted for a bit longer before disconnecting the call.

It was two weeks now from the time he landed in Mumbai…

A deep sigh shuddered through Advik's being. He could understand his grandfather's stubbornness. But even his grandmother, Akshatha Hegde, didn't seem to be interested in communicating with him.

Damn it! What was it that he had done? Was going abroad for further education such a big sin? Advik wanted to smash something. After staying in the hotel for a couple of days, Advik had found this apartment not far from the Hegde household in Bandra. Just a few buildings away, actually.

He could clearly see how his grandfather kept control over his family as well as his business. He had complete hold over the purse strings. Both his sons were dependent on him financially, despite working long hours at the restaurant. Ganesh and Kartik slogged their asses off. While they had plenty of clothes and even a luxury car for each one of them; they still had very less spending money. Advik's mother, Vrunda, had a hundred *tolas* of gold jewellery and a wardrobe full of exorbitant silk saris. But she had but a couple of thousands of rupees in her purse at any given time.

As for Advik, he had been his grandparents' pet child. Akshatha used to give him pocket money in secret. Even Bhaskar wasn't averse to giving his grandson some spending money when he was at school. Later, when Advik began to work at the restaurant, he had demanded and gotten away with an excellent salary that he had saved in a separate account. Ultimately, it was his own savings that had funded his education, along with an education loan he had taken from a bank. The loan was almost paid off, what with Advik working really hard for more than three years after completing his course in New York.

And here he was, living in a rented apartment, having a really good job with the popular restaurant chain. He swore to himself that he would show his grandfather that Advik wasn't one to buckle under emotional blackmail.

That first evening back in Mumbai…

When Ganesh arrived at the hotel to meet his son, he brought along with him an olive branch from

Bhaskar. But of course, it was conditional. "Your *Ajja* wouldn't mind if you work with us at Mysuru Ahara. He…"

"What?" Advik lifted a supercilious brow, forgetting for a moment that it was his father who was in front of him and not his arrogant and stubborn grandfather. "So, *Ajja* wants me to work in his restaurant? Are you sure?"

Ganesh gave his son an eager smile. He was really keen that the rift between grandfather and grandson should be healed. "Yes, Advik. He is even ready to pay you a salary."

Advik stared at his father, feeling rather sorry for him. It looked like his grandfather wanted to manipulate him even if he didn't want his grandson to live under the same roof as the rest of the family. "Dad." He placed a hand on his father's shoulder, turning to give his mother a wink. "Listen, Dad. Do you really think I am going to waste my time at Mysuru Ahara after training for two years in global cuisine? And gaining so many years of experience in western restaurants? Does it make any kind of sense, Dad?"

Ganesh's mouth drooped at the corners. He couldn't deny his son's logic. But he felt so torn. Shaking his head, he sat back on the chair in his son's hotel room, his shoulders slouched in defeat.

Vrunda had a difficult time holding back her tears. She had been so looking forward to her son's return from his sojourn abroad; eager to welcome him back into the family. But her father-in-law had thrown a spanner in the works. Though thoroughly miffed with the old man, there was nothing she could do about the situation. After all, in the Hegde household, it was the men who ruled; especially the one at the top. Biting her lip to stop the tears from flowing, she leaned her head against her son's shoulder. How she had missed him!

His parents only left when they realised that Advik was sleeping on his feet, worn out by jet lag. Extremely tired, he lay down on the comfortable bed, his mind churning at the unexpected turn his life had taken. All because of his grandfather's obstinate behaviour.

Fuck you, old man!

6

Kartik paced the balcony outside his bedroom restlessly. It was two weeks since his nephew had returned from the USA. And Advik had not stepped inside the family home once. He had been shocked when he had found out from Advik's mother—his sister-in-law Vrunda—that his nephew had been banned from entering the family home.

Even now, after fifteen days, Kartik fumed, his frustration knowing no bounds. Advik was Bhaskar Hegde's only grandchild, damn it! How could the old man do what he was doing?

He couldn't help recalling the time—it was in the year 1995—when his parents had stopped him from getting married to the love of his life... Janani...

Kartik Hegde stood at the window of his room, looking down at the sea crashing against the shore. The waves appeared to reflect his state of mind as he recalled his conversation with his father barely a couple of hours ago.

"Kartik..." He heard his mother Akshatha's voice call him. It was dinner time and the family ate together, at least those who were at home at eight in the evening. His elder brother Ganesh was at Madras Meals, a sprawling restaurant of two thousand square feet nowadays, set in the heart of Matunga. It was actually one thousand square feet since space was scarce in the area. But they had managed to create an A/C section on the mezzanine, doubling the area in the bargain.

A soft smile appeared on Kartik's lips when he thought of Ramani Iyer, his father's partner. The man was a business whiz and really knew how to go about getting the lawmen on his side. He also kept an iron control over the income and expenditure and was completely trustworthy.

His father, Bhaskar Hegde, was no less. While Bhaskar preferred to don the chef's hat more often, he also kept track of the business, though the pressure was less on him thanks to his shrewd partner.

An inadvertent sigh escaped Kartik, his lean frame shuddering in reaction. He was in love with Janani Iyer, Ramani's daughter and youngest child. And the best part was that she returned his feelings.

But…

Kartik rammed his fist into the wall near the window, almost breaking the bones on his right hand when he thought of his father's reaction to the news...

"*Appa…*" Kartik had walked into his father's room at five in the evening. Bhaskar usually came home for a siesta before he went back to the restaurant in the evening. Though he still enjoyed creating drool worthy dishes, there were four cooks who had Madras Meals' kitchen running smoothly.

"What is it, Kartik?" asked Bhaskar, looking at his strapping younger son up and down, a typical scowl on his face. Even at fifty-nine, he had a head full of hair, though it was liberally spread with grey. He sported a thick moustache that he was very proud of.

"*Appa,* I wanted to talk to you about…" Kartik hesitated, glancing at his mother who walked in with a tray containing two sets of *tabara* and *tumbler,* in a typical South Indian style, steam wafting from them, bringing the aroma of filter coffee into the room.

Akshatha was already aware of what Kartik wanted to tell his father and she was quite unhappy about the matter. She refused to look in her son's direction as she placed the tray on a table beside the bed.

Taking a deep breath, Kartik continued valiantly, "*Appa,* I would like to marry…"

Bhaskar raised a shaggy brow at his son. "Marry? Whom? Why the hurry? Can't you wait for your parents to find you a bride?" He turned to glare at his wife who shrugged, refusing to join the conversation.

"I love Janani, *Appa*. I want to marry her. Will you please speak to Ramani uncle…?"

"What?" Bhaskar kept his coffee tumbler down with a clatter as he glared at his son. "Have you taken leave of your senses? We are Kannada brahmins and they are Tamil. How did you even imagine that I would agree to this idea?" He turned to glare at his wife once again. "Did you know about this? Why didn't you tell me that your son has such a foolish idea?" The questions tumbled out of Bhaskar's mouth in a rapid fire.

Kartik frowned, his face resembling his father's more than ever. It wasn't as if Bhaskar's sons didn't have freedom—to an extent. It was just that marriage was a big decision, the coming together of not just the bride and groom but their respective families too. Well, his father's bark was always worse than his bite.

"Please *Appa,* you and Ramani uncle have been close friends and partners for more than thirty years. Doesn't that count more than you both belonging to different territories of India? And after all, both are brahmins at the end of the day. Okay, we speak different mother tongues, but then, we converse in Hindi and English most of the time. Please think about it, *Appa*. I love her and Janani loves me too." Kartik spoke in a soft and pacifying voice, hoping to win his father over. Having said his bit, he picked up a tumbler of coffee and drank from it.

Bhaskar looked from his wife to his son and then back again. "What is he saying, Akshatha? Has your son gone mad?"

"I don't know," said Akshatha, a pained expression on her face, "I can't understand this modern generation and their so-called love marriage. They see all kinds of stupid films and want to live like the hero and heroine in those. I told him that I am not for this idea. You and Ramani *anna* have a business partnership. Okay, you both are friends and our families are close. That doesn't mean we can become relatives too." She spoke fast without taking a breath, her words falling over each other as she gave her opinion.

"Ganesh married the woman we chose for him, didn't he?" asked Bhaskar rhetorically before turning to Kartik. "Your brother is happily married to Vrunda, or isn't he?" He asked his younger born who nodded pathetically. "Well then, you have your answer there." He turned to walk towards the bathroom, to freshen up before leaving for Madras Meals.

"That's not the point, is it *Appa*?" Kartik's voice rose by a few decibels as his temper came to the fore. "Ganesh wasn't in love with any girl and hence didn't mind marrying the girl you chose for him. But I love Janani. She's the only one I want to marry. I will never marry anyone else." He gave both his parents a defiant look before stepping out of the room to go up the stairs of their Bandra duplex and into his room.

And now, after a few hours, his mother was calling out to him to go down for dinner as if nothing had happened. No, Kartik didn't want to join his family at the dining table just now. He simply wasn't in the mood to pretend that everything was fine. Coming to a quick decision, he changed into formal clothes and walked out of his room, down the stairs and out of their house without telling anyone anything.

"*Appa*, I want to talk to you," said Janani, a wide smile on her lovely face as she addressed her father, Ramani. Confidence oozed from her as she walked up to her father and sat down on the corner of the table where he was sitting and working on accounts. "Why have you brought your work home, *Appa*? Aren't you working hard enough at the restaurant?" she asked him as she eyed the big account ledgers.

Ramani removed his reading glasses and rubbed his eyes before smiling at his daughter. "You know me, Janu. I love my work too much. But you tell me, what is it?" He looked at his youngest child with adoration in his eyes. At twenty, she was the apple of his eye.

"Er…*Appa,* I…" Colour ran up Janani's soft and rounded cheeks as sudden shyness overtook her. While she chatted with her father about everything under the sun, this was the first time she was going to confess to him about the love of her life. Taking a deep breath to garner her confidence, she lifted her gaze to look into her father's eyes before saying, "*Appa,* I'm in love."

Ramani looked startled at first before he laughed, clapping his hands. "And who's the lucky man?" he asked.

Wild colour suffused Janani's face once again as she said in a whisper, "It's Kartik, *Appa*."

"What? Kartik *Appa*? Who's this now? I can't think of…"

"*Appa*!" Janani jumped off the corner of the desk and stamped her foot. "Stop teasing me. You know who I am talking about."

"Do I? I don't know…"

Janani stamped her foot yet again. "I love Kartik Hegde, your best friend's son," she declared loudly, glaring at her father with her huge dark eyes.

Ramani laughed heartily, taking his daughter's hand to shake it vigorously. "You have excellent taste, my child. Kartik is a smart fellow and is handsome too. So, shall I talk to his parents tomorrow itself? And fix your marriage to him?"

Janani gave her father a small nod, too choked with emotion to say anything, before running out of Ramani's study, his laughter following her.

Janani and Kartik met at the corner of a narrow lane not far from Madras Meals. He picked her up in his fiat car and they took off in the direction of Juhu.

"Are you upset about something, Kartik?" asked Janani, looking at him with love shining in her eyes.

Kartik didn't remove his gaze off the road as he replied, "It's my father."

"Why, what happened?" It was with great difficulty that Janani kept a curb on the excitement that was bubbling inside her. She wanted to tell him about how her father thought that Kartik would make a smart and suitable husband for her. But not now. Something had happened to upset Kartik.

Kartik drove on until they reached Juhu Chowpatty, not all that far from the Palm Grove Hotel. Stopping the car, he killed the engine before turning and looking at Janani's face. She looked adorable and his heart beat double time when he took in her lovely features. A deep sigh shuddered through him as he took her hands in his. "I spoke to my father, Janani. He insists that we can't marry. He..." Kartik took a deep breath to stop his voice from breaking before continuing, "he says that we belong to different communities and cannot get together."

Janani's hold on his hands tightened as she squeezed them reassuringly. "I think you shouldn't worry too much. My dad thinks it's a great idea. In fact, he thinks you are handsome and smart and will be the perfect husband for me." Colour rushed up her cheeks as she said the words, her eyes studying his sad face avidly.

Kartik shook his head. "My father will never agree." He gritted his teeth in anger when he replayed the conversation of that evening yet again.

Janani lifted a hand to caress his rough cheek. "Relax Kartik. Let my father talk to yours tomorrow. What do we know? It might work out better than we expect." She was always positive that things would work out for the best.

Kartik gave her a pathetic look, not having her confidence. He sighed once again, saying, "Maybe. Let's see." He had been going to suggest that they elope. But then, looking at her, it didn't seem fair. She was used to leading a luxurious life, as the most favourite of Ramani Iyer's children. And the man was rich.

Well, his father was rich too. But Bhaskar Hegde was tight fisted and gave his sons just enough to survive. Since both of the sons were involved in the family business, all the income remained in the family account. At the end of it all, Kartik had only a minimum balance in his personal bank account.

"Cheer up, Kartik," said Janani, opening the car door. "I want to have some *bhel puri*. Are you going to join me?"

Unable to share her enthusiasm for *chaat* or any kind of food for that matter, Kartik got out of the car with reluctance and followed her towards the long line of food stalls that offered all kinds of street foods that Bombay was famous for—from *pani puri* to *sev puri* to *pav bhaji* and sandwiches. Despite being a week night, people thronged the area, eager to gorge on the delicious offerings after having spent the evening at the beach.

Janani insisted on feeding morsels into the reluctant Kartik's mouth, even as she gave him reassuring smiles. Not that they melted his hardened heart. He had no hope as far as his parents were concerned. And elopement wasn't an option. He was too level-headed to consider it.

After many attempts, Janani gave up trying to cheer her boyfriend up, the smile disappearing from her face that was aching by now. "Let's go back, Kartik," she said.

Giving her a small nod, the silent Kartik took her hand to guide her towards the car, his shoulders drooped in defeat.

It came about that Kartik's negativity was more powerful than Janani's positive excitement. An argument ensued between the two close friends, Ramani and Bhaskar when the former went to the Hegdes' residence to ask for Kartik's hand for his daughter.

Ramani's wife, Savitri, wasn't all that keen about the idea. For one, she didn't get along very well with Bhaskar's wife Akshatha. While Savitri was from a middleclass background, Akshatha's parents were millionaires. Bhaskar Hegde's wife tended to look down her sharp nose at Ramani Iyer's wife. While the families met socially at least once a month, the wives kept away from one another, managing to just share a vague smile in greeting.

"*Enna*, can't we find any other groom for our Janu? Why do you want to get her married to Akshatha's son? That woman is too proud, arrogant actually." Savitri shuddered as she imagined having the other woman for her *sammandhi*. "Our daughter is beautiful and well educated. If you let word get around that we are looking for a suitable groom, there will be a long line of people knocking at our door." There was immense pride in the mother's voice as she spoke of her youngest child.

Ramani grinned at his wife, nodding. "I agree, Savitri. But then, Janu is in love with that boy Kartik. Isn't it only right that we get her married to him?"

Savitri looked at her husband with shocked eyes gone wide, her hands on her cheeks as she held her jaw even as it dropped. "Love? What nonsense is this? How can you allow our daughter to do such a thing? She's so young. She..."

Ramani burst out laughing. "Did you hear yourself speak just now, Savitri? I didn't *allow* our daughter to do anything. It was she who came and told me that she's in love."

"Shameless chit!" Savitri grimaced. "She had the gall to come and tell you, her father, that she's in love? It looks like I've brought her up badly."

Ramani continued to laugh. "You have to admit that our daughter's smart. Or she might have confessed her love to you and imagine what would have happened if that were the case." He guffawed, amused more than ever as he looked at the angry expression on his wife's face. "Come on, Savitri, cheer up. Kartik is a good boy and will make Janu a wonderful husband."

"But his mother is such a pain," she wailed, glaring at her husband.

"You find her painful. But it's not you who's going to live in their home, right?" asked Ramani logically.

Savitri turned her face away from him, her body stiff with anger. "I don't like this idea. But then, when have you listened to me, ever?"

Ramani sighed as he walked to her and laid a hand on her shoulder. "Come on, Savitri. That's not fair. I always consult you about everything. Even this, I am keen to pursue only because Janu is interested in Kartik. It's not as if I want our daughter to marry my best friend's son."

Savitri turned tearful eyes to her husband. "*Ennamo pongo*! I'm not very happy about this. But I accept that you know best."

The effervescent Ramani gave her one more grin as he patted his wife's cheek. "Believe me, everything happens for the best."

So, the Iyer couple visited the Hegde home on Wednesday, the weekly holiday at Madras Meals.

After having the coffee and snacks—*Mysore pak*, made of *besan*, ghee and sugar; and *Jeegujje bonda*, breadfruit fritters; with spicy green chilly chutney—the four of them—Bhaskar, Akshatha, Ramani and Savitri—sat down on the balcony to chat.

It was only the men who actually talked while the women kept glowering at each other, their dislike unhidden.

"Okay, let me come to the point of our visit, Bhaskar," said Ramani, rubbing his hands together, "you know my daughter, Janani. She..."

Akshatha's face turned stony while Bhaskar's appeared confused, though both immediately guessed what Ramani was getting at.

"Er... of course I know Janani. Your daughter is not only beautiful, but intelligent too," said Bhaskar, meaning every word he said.

Ramani gave him a proud smile. "I was thinking... why not get your son Kartik and Janani married?" He lifted a dark eyebrow at his friend.

Bhaskar gave his wife a quick look. When Kartik had spoken to him about the alliance, it had been different. But now that Ramani was asking him directly, he wasn't sure how to refuse him. But then, they both belonged to different communities. He felt kind of torn.

Akshatha glared at Savitri as if it was all her mistake before turning to look at her husband. What was wrong with the man? Hadn't they discussed the matter only the other day when Kartik had told them about his love for the Iyer girl? She nudged her husband, commanding him with her eyes to refuse the alliance.

Bhaskar was in a quandary. How could he be rude to his friend? After all, they had grown too close over the past three decades. But then, he also knew how much his wife disliked Mrs Iyer. Tch! What an awkward situation!

"Er… let me talk to my wife and son and get back to you on this, Ramani," he said now, unable to say an outright no.

"What is there to talk?" asked Akshatha, her voice shrill as she glowered at her husband. "We are Kannadigas and they are Tamils." She turned to look at Ramani and said, "Ramani *anna*, how can you ask us about this? You are as orthodox as we are."

Ramani laid a hand on his wife's arm as Savitri was all set to burst out. Speaking softly and persuasively, he said, "I agree with you, Akshatha madam. But we are all from the old generation. Nowadays, the children think differently. My daughter Janani told me that she's in love with your son Kartik. Would you have spoken to your father on such a matter when you were that age? That's how much the world has changed." There was pride in his voice and face when Ramani spoke of his favourite child.

Akshatha gave him such a demeaning glance as if he was dirt stuck under her shoe. "That just goes to show how badly your daughter has been brought up. But then, I don't expect any better from Janani considering that she has Mrs Iyer for her mother."

All hell broke loose as Savitri pushed back her chair noisily to stand up, her face red with humiliation. "How dare you?" she snarled at the other woman.

Bhaskar pressed a hand on his wife's shoulder to try to stop her from speaking further. But his gesture only seemed to instigate both the women all the more.

A slanging match ensued between the two women which lasted for the next fifteen minutes, not letting either man get a word in. All the poison the two of them had held within themselves from the day they met for the first time, came to the fore as they shouted and screamed at one another, calling each other names in their mother tongues, making Ramani and Bhasker squirm and wince in turns.

Within the week, the long-time friends and business partners split up, having no recourse but to go their separate ways as their wives had torn everything to tatters. Now, there was no way that Ramani and Bhaskar could run a hotel together, let alone get their children married to each other.

Ramani Iyer paid ten lakh rupees to Bhaskar Hegde to retain the premises as well as the brand of Madras Meals while the latter opened Mysuru Ahara, just one lane away from the original hotel within two months of the separation.

As for Kartik Hegde and Janani Iyer, the two dug in their feet and insisted on spending the rest of their lives as bachelors. No amount of persuasion by their respective fathers or tantrums thrown by their mothers could convince either of them to marry someone they did not love.

And hence, from 1995, Matunga sported two stellar restaurants instead of one—Madras Meals and Mysuru Ahara—both in high demand. Both the restaurants continued to serve Kannada and Tamil cuisine, most of the dishes similar. Customers continued to throng both restaurants, queuing up outside the portals during the weekends.

But the rift between the Iyers and the Hegdes had become too wide to be breached. Even while passing each other on the Matunga lanes, the one-time friends didn't even bother to acknowledge each other. They became the biggest rivals in the restaurant business in that area over the years.

Kartik came to the present with a deep sigh…

He caught glimpses of Janani whenever she passed him on the street, which was rare. After all, she wasn't interested in the restaurant business, but had gone on to become an artist.

He collected every single article printed by the newspapers, all about Janani's art and fame. In the beginning, he had spent a lot of sleepless nights thinking of the love of his life. But over time, he had learned to live his life. But deep down, he couldn't help a feeling of resentment towards both his parents for not letting him live his life the way he wanted.

A gentle smile spread across his face when his thoughts returned to his nephew. Kartik was truly glad that Advik wasn't making the same mistake that his uncle had made. The boy had managed to slip out of the Hegde patriarch's stranglehold.

God bless you, my child! Kartik blessed his nephew from the bottom of his heart.

7

Aaradhya had completed all the basic baking for the next day, leaving the cake bases, breads and croissants to cool down in the kitchen. She planned to pack them all away for the night after an hour or so. In the meanwhile, she was working on her laptop, planning the dessert menu for the coming week.

There was also the new idea she was working on—a café serving global cuisine. Not just that, but one which catered to vegans. This was a project really close to her heart. Always having been vegetarian, she had been reading up a lot about veganism and was finding the subject more and more fascinating as she learned all about it. *What the Health*, a documentary on Netflix, had finally nailed it for her.

Aaradhya was so far convinced about veganism theoretically, and was yet to become a vegan herself. Maybe sometime in the future. As of now, she was too fond of cottage cheese and *more kozhambu*—a gravy made from beaten curd—to want to give up all animal products.

But even as she worked, there was a major distraction for Aaradhya—in the form of the Tinder app. Okay, not the whole app per se, but one particular account. She was simply not interested in the likes and Super Likes she had been steadily receiving from the time she opened her account. Okay, maybe not all that many, but definitely more than ten to fifteen per week.

As for Advik, it was a wonder that he, who had remained pretty much of a recluse during their trip back to Mumbai, had reached out to her via the Tinder chat box. Which had given her a lot of hope. She had been sure that they would be able to pursue a relationship.

Only to realise that it was just her wild imagination which had arrived at that conclusion. The reality was simply bullshit!

She had taken great hope when he had pinged her on the Tinder chat box first. In fact, she had been quivering with excitement when she noticed that she had a message from him. But the chat had ended abruptly. It looked like he had only wanted to confirm that she was also interested in food and cooking. And nothing after that.

How the hell was it possible to hold a one-sided conversation? Grr… Aaradhya gritted her teeth before opening the app to check if he had posted any new pictures.

She sat up straight even as her heart played ping pong in her chest, clogging her throat.

Oh my God! Oh my God! Oh my God!

No one had the right to look so damn delectable! Okay, the main part of the picture was taken up by a steaming sizzler. But it was the man behind the counter who drew her attention. A pristine white apron fell down from his neck to wherever the hell it ended. She couldn't know as the photo covered the area down to his hips. He was holding a chef's cap in his left hand, his longish hair all mussed up and falling over his forehead. His eyes reminded her of melting chocolate and they were smiling for the camera.

All her adult years, Aaradhya had not been attracted to a man wearing a moustache. She actually had an aversion for them, or so she had believed until she set sight on Advik. His handlebar moustache only seemed to add to his charm as it bracketed the corners of his damn sexy lips. And as for his dimples, they made her want to swoon.

Aaradhya placed a hand over the left side of her chest, as if to ease the pressure there. Damn! *How I wish I could go and meet him right now!*

She quickly opened the chat box and typed, without thinking too much.

Hey! That sizzler looks so appetising! Which one is it?

She waited and she waited… and she waited some more. Okay, it wasn't as if she stopped working to stare into her Tinder account. But she kept going back every few minutes; or was it every few seconds? Whatever! She kept checking her phone a number of times, even as she packed away the goodies she had baked; jotted down many points on her Excel Worksheet before shutting down her laptop… but still there was no response from Advik.

It was a wonder that her teeth didn't fall off, the way she gritted her jaw. Damn the man! In a fit of temper, she switched off her phone. She had to, or she might have driven herself mad that night.

She fell on her bed and waited in vain for sleep to claim her. Aaradhya wasn't sure when she actually went to sleep before the ping of her phone woke her up. Checking the time, she was startled to note that it was past five in the morning.

In a fit of restlessness, she had switched her phone back on when sleep had refused to come the earlier night. But she had forgotten to switch her phone to silent mode as was her usual habit.

Opening the phone to find out what the ping was all about, Aaradhya received a pleasant shock. It was an update on her Tinder app. Quickly opening it to her chat box, she grinned foolishly when she saw there was a reply from Advik.

Hey, long time no see. It's a paneer shaslik sizzler. You like?

With her grin turning wider even as her heart jumped with joy, Aaradhya typed quickly with both her thumbs.

I love paneer. Where do I get to taste your sizzler?

She didn't give a damn that it sounded as if she was inviting herself to sample his cooking. What the hell! She was doing exactly that.

Don't know. Will ping you if an opportunity turns up, for sure.

Aaradhya grimaced at his response. He couldn't have been any less enthusiastic than that. Fuming, she locked the phone, switching it to silent mode before falling back on her bed.

He was going to ping her **IF** an opportunity turned up. And what were the chances of such an occasion happening, ever? She didn't have any kind of faith in that vague promise.

I suppose it's a wonder that he had replied, at all. She banged both her fists on her pillow, doing her best to fluff it up before burying her face in it.

Why can't I accept that Advik isn't interested in me?

While Aaradhya wanted to kick herself, she realised that she wasn't ready to give up, not so easily. Come on, the man was totally drool worthy for one thing. And for another, she couldn't forget the sizzling chemistry that had made her flesh break out in goose bumps whenever she went within a few feet of him. And damn it all! It had never, but never happened to her before.

How can I ignore something like that?!

It wasn't even as though Advik was the handsomest of all the men she had met in her life. No! Aaradhya had met more than her fair share of attractive men, some of whom had even shown a deep interest in her. But this was the first time she had felt her heart race when she was in the proximity of an adult male.

And I had to fall for the silent type! Probably an introvert at that! Grr… Aaradhya hit her pillow some more before turning to lie down facing the other side. *Sleep!* She commanded herself, not really surprised to find out even that simple aspect of her life had gone out of her control.

Advik was smiling as he sipped from his mug of coffee, even as he scrolled through the Tinder app on his phone. The picture with the sizzler was a super hit. More than that, it had given him great satisfaction to play chef at the one of Hot Foods' restaurants. He had literally cooked up a storm at the all-day diner, loving every minute of it. The customers had all left with a satisfied smile on their faces. Many of them had asked to take a selfie with the chef. And Advik had obliged, every one of them. The picture which he had posted on Tinder had been clicked from his phone camera by one of those ecstatic customers.

And it looked as if Aaradhya liked the picture too. Though she had commented only about the sizzler and not him. Well, and whose fault was that? He gave a soft sigh as he bent down to tie the laces of his sport shoes. The plan was to go for a long run and he was glad that he had finally managed to wake up early after returning to Mumbai.

What with the jet lag, change in time zones and hectic work schedule that tended to get erratic on most days, he had not had a chance to go for a run, his favourite way to keep fit. All these days, he had been managing by doing some light exercises and stretches every day.

He got out of his apartment and took the staircase from the seventh floor instead of the lift, breathing in deeply of the early morning air when he stepped outside the gate, jogging for a few minutes before he reached the Carter Road promenade. Jogging along the path, he was happy to note that there were only a few early risers who were walking or running on the path. Even as he jogged steadily along, his thoughts went back to Aaradhya.

Sigh!!!

Why can't I just forget her?

It wasn't as if he had known her for a long time. They had spent a brief time together, and had not even had much of a conversation between them. Yes, she had found him on Tinder. But it was he who had begun to chat with her on the app.

Damn!

Advik went up to a tea vendor across the road and ordered for a cup. While waiting, he bought a newspaper from the nearby stand and glanced his way through it. There was nothing of interest as he read the headlines even as he sipped from his glass of tea. Paying the vendor, he rolled the newspaper in one hand before walking towards home.

Should I meet her, maybe just once?

Advik was sorely tempted as he recalled her charcoal gaze and pouty lips. Aaradhya was definitely hot looking and he so wanted to see her again. Maybe he could make her understand that he had a hectic schedule and didn't have time for a girlfriend. And maybe she would accept that as she was in the same profession.

He snapped his fingers! Yes! That was it! If she was as keen about her career as he was, then she would definitely be able to relate to his sentiments. Perfect!

He quickly typed into his Tinder chat box.

Possible to meet for dinner this evening?

He waited for her response which didn't come for a couple of hours. When his phone pinged, Advik dropped the spatula, switching off the gas stove before rushing to pick his phone. It must be Aaradhya, he was sure of it.

He opened Tinder to see her response.

A latish dinner works? I can be free only by nine.

He quickly typed his reply.

Perfect! Can you meet me at High Street Phoenix? The pizza place at the Palladium? BTW, I have an hour's dinner break but will have to get back to work after that.

When do you get off work?

11

I'll get there by 9.30, okay?

See you

He added a smiley face for good measure, his heart dancing with joy. Advik realised that it was the first time he was feeling happy after returning home to Mumbai. Maybe meeting Aaradhya would be a good thing.

No! Not a good thing! But the best thing that could happen to him at present.

Whistling tunelessly, Advik went back to cook his breakfast.

8

Aaradhya's heart beat loudly as she got into her car—an ink blue Suzuki Ignis—her hands trembling when she placed them on the steering wheel. She couldn't stop the silly grin that split her face as she set the car in motion.

Finally! Finally, she was going to meet the handsome Advik for dinner. The man who set her heart pumping even when she was simply gazing at his pictures. She hummed to herself along with her stereo and it wasn't long before she reached the parking area at the mall in Lower Parel. Getting out of the car, she locked it before going inside and taking the escalator. She was a few minutes late, but that didn't really matter. She planned to wait until he finished at work anyway. And today, she was determined to find out all there was to know about the man.

With a determined thrust to her small chin and the light of battle shining in her eyes, Aaradhya pushed the panelled glass door to enter the Italian joint, looking to her left and then to her right as she searched for his familiar face.

"Hey!" Advik lifted his hand in greeting when he saw Aaradhya step inside the restaurant. Was she a sight for sore eyes! As she walked closer, he couldn't help thinking that she looked gorgeous in pristine white form fitting cotton pants teamed with a black t-shirt that had the words TINDER LOVING CARE printed in white across her chest. Dragging his gaze away from her long and slim legs was a task. And he couldn't stop the grin that surfaced on his face when he read the words before bringing his thumb and index finger together in appreciation. "How have you been?" he asked.

"Not too bad, I suppose. Though I'm feeling way happier now that I've met you," she said boldly, checking him out from the top of his sleek head all the way down to the sneakers on his feet. She was glad to note that the apron was missing though he wore a bright blue t-shirt which had the brand logo of the Italian restaurant entwined with the Hot Foods logo on the front. He had teamed it with dark blue jeans. "No cooking today?" she asked before he could respond.

He would have replied if he hadn't been busy catching the breath which had left him gasping on hearing her words. *Did I hear what I did just now?* Advik gave her a wary glance and wasn't really surprised when she met his gaze head on.

So! She had wanted to meet him! As much as he had wanted to meet her, if not more. Aaradhya was bold and beautiful! Just the kind of woman he liked. He swallowed the groan that welled up in his throat. *What have I done, inviting her for dinner?*

Slowly shaking his head, he replied, "Nope! Today I'm just the manager at this outlet."

"Hmm…" She looked around appreciatively at the cheerful restaurant decorated in bright blue and pastel yellow. "This looks nice."

He tilted his head in a nod before taking her elbow firmly to turn her in the direction of the table reserved for them. He realised his mistake the moment his fingers came in contact with the soft skin of her inner elbow. Damn! The blood sizzled in his veins, all the way from his fingers to the rest of his body, making his body hair stand up in attention. Advik was startled to note that no woman he had dated so far had ever had such a deep physical impact on him.

I am a goner!

Aaradhya revelled in his touch, the smile on her face deepening as she turned her head to gaze up at his profile. She had known that his touch would affect her. But… awareness swept through her body, tightening her nerves even as she felt her breasts swell, their tips puckering into tight buds. She would have never believed it possible if someone had told her that her body could react this way to a man's touch on her elbow of all places.

Advik looked straight, refusing to acknowledge her gaze on his profile, the one that he was too aware of. After all, hadn't he felt the heat gushing into his face when she turned around to look at him?

Stepping to the table for two, he pulled out the chair and waited for her to sit down before taking the other one. It was a few seconds before he could gather his breath to speak normally; at least as close to normal as was possible under the circumstances. "Would you like to have a gin and tonic?" he asked, recalling her preference from their time in Delhi.

She smiled into his eyes, pleased to know that he hadn't forgotten. "Yes, please. Only one, though. I have my car with me and don't want to get drunk."

Her hoarse voice played on his heartstrings, making his body tighten with need. Maybe it was because he hadn't been to bed with a woman in three months. *That must be it,* he told himself, the reason why she had such a profound effect on his person. Giving her a nod, he lifted a hand to the waiter.

"What can I get you, sir?" asked the man.

"A gin and tonic for the lady, Savio; and a beer for me."

"Sure, sir. Any starters?" asked Savio politely.

Advik lifted an eyebrow at Aaradhya, staring at her with mesmerised eyes, his throat drying up at he studied her lovely face. Her large, almond-shaped eyes appeared darker than ever, framed by long and curling eyelashes, her eyebrows shaped like wings below a wide forehead. As for her nose, it was slim and sharp, framed by slim cheeks ending in a sharp chin. Her lips were rosy coloured and moist, inadvertently inviting him to take a closer look even as they made him wonder how they would feel under his own. Smothering another groan, he asked her in a gruff voice, "I'd recommend the basil tomato soup if you would like to have it with some garlic bread. Or maybe bruschetta. What do you think?"

"Mmm… I think I'll go with the bruschetta along with my drink. Maybe we can order the soup later?"

"Right!" He turned to the waiter and placed the order for a serving of bruschetta topped with pesto sauce and roasted bell peppers, both red and yellow.

"I'm so glad you invited me to dinner." Aaradhya spoke the moment Savio stepped away from their table, her eyes shining with merriment. "I've been dying to meet you. I…"

Advik lifted a hand to stop her from speaking further. "Aara, listen. I…" he paused, wondering how to tell her that he was not just busy, but his whole life was complicated right now. And he had to somehow let her know that without being hurtful or insulting. "I've taken up a job that takes up most of my waking hours. That's why I…"

She nodded vigorously. "I realise how busy you are after seeing you here today, at your workplace," she said, sweeping her gaze around her. "You not only manage the restaurants, but you also step in when the chef takes an unscheduled off, right?" She had read about the role of chef and manager for Hot Foods on their website when she searched for the information on Google.

He gave a sigh before nodding, finally sitting back in his chair, doing his best to relax. He had done his best to keep her out of his life. But it had become next to impossible after they connected on Tinder. Even then, he had really tried over the past few weeks. This was it! He couldn't resist Aaradhya anymore and he was simply going to let the future take care of itself.

Nothing to beat it if they could have a relationship that worked for both of them. He sighed! But it would take nothing less than a magic formula is what he believed.

At least, it looked like she did understand that his career took up most of his waking hours. As long as Aaradhya didn't expect him to be available whenever she was free. He would have to wait and watch where it took them.

But even Advik didn't foresee the speed at which their relationship developed from that evening on.

9

Advik leaned back in his seat, enjoying the soft instrumental music from the car stereo, as he watched Aaradhya drive her car skilfully, unaware of the almost sappy smile on his face. And why not? Usually, a company car dropped him home. Today, he had cancelled it when Aaradhya offered to drive him home.

Despite all the anxiety he had undergone before agreeing to meet her, their dinner date had gone off really well. They could converse pretty comfortably as they chatted about the various culinary courses they had attended abroad, apart from other things. It looked like both of them had taken a keen interest in cooking right from a young age. There were no uncomfortable pauses when they conversed, as if they had known each other for a long time instead of the brief spell they had spent together during their travel back to Mumbai.

So, here he was, sitting back in the passenger seat, completely relaxed. Their first date had gone without a hitch and it should be over when she dropped him at his building's gate. And without any untoward incident too! Not that he had expected anything to go wrong. Just that, she was a walking, talking temptation to any man, let alone Advik. The trick was to resist the attraction and somehow, he had managed to survive the evening.

Phew!

And there had been no suggestion of another date. He didn't plan to talk about it, most definitely not. As for Aaradhya, well, she hadn't mentioned it all this long. Hence the chances were high that she wouldn't do it, not tonight at least.

"Take the left there," he said, pointing a finger in the direction.

"Okay," she responded, turning the car to the left. She followed his instructions and it wasn't long before they reached the building compound where he lived. She drove through the open gates, ignoring the look of enquiry on Advik's face. It was obvious that he had expected her to drop him outside. *As if he can get rid of me so easily,* she thought to herself, smiling.

Noticing the sign for 'visitors' parking', she manoeuvred the car efficiently between a Hyundai i20 and a Volvo SUV before bringing it to a stop.

Advik lifted an enquiring eyebrow at her even as he removed his seat belt, rather surprised to see her doing the same.

"Aren't you going to offer me a cup of coffee?" she asked, lifting a challenging eyebrow at him. Not waiting for his reply, she opened the door on her side and stepped out.

Holding back his falling jaw, he stepped outside as well before looking at her above the roof of the car.

"It's kind of late, isn't it?" he asked. After all, it was past midnight.

"So? I am not Cinderella," she said, with a defiant tilt to her chin.

Unable to help himself, he threw back his head and laughed out loud.

Aaradhya stared at him, her eyes wide as she looked at the long line of his throat, his Adam's apple bobbing as he laughed hard. How was it possible that he grew handsomer each time she set eyes on him?

Catching her avid gaze from the corner of his eyes, Advik quickly sobered up to look at her. "Seriously, Aara. It's late. I…"

"…have to be at work by noon tomorrow. So, what's the rush? You don't seem all that sleepy to me. Come on, Advik. Take me to your home." It was an effort not to stamp her foot in impatience.

She had him there. Advik grimaced. And it was he who had told her all about his working hours. Unlike a lot of people, it looked like Aaradhya actually listened.

"Come along! We aren't exactly achieving anything standing here in the car park, are we?" She placed her hand on his forearm, turning him towards the building.

Her proximity drove him crazy with longing, her head touching his shoulder as they walked side by side towards the elevator.

"Which floor are you in?" she asked as they waited for the lift.

"Seventh," he answered briefly, looking everywhere but at her lovely face. He gave a sigh of relief when the lift arrived at the ground floor. Opening the doors, he waited for her to get inside before stepping right behind her. Was he glad that it was big enough to hold eight people?! He couldn't remain far enough away from the gorgeous woman who made his body thrum with desire.

He opened the door to his flat and was glad that the living room was in a fairly decent condition, with no discarded clothes lying on the sofas or the centre table. Phew! He quickly walked ahead of her to pick up the bath towel he had thrown in one corner. Opening the door to the wash area, he threw it in the washing machine before stepping back into the hall.

Aaradhya stood not far from the entrance, her eyes following her reluctant host's movements. She was torn between amusement and a deep sense of attraction that made her want to fling herself into his arms. What would he do if she did exactly that?

Before she could reach a conclusion, Advik walked back to where she was standing and said, "Why don't you sit down? I'll go make coffee." Without waiting for her response, he did an about turn and walked left, where she presumed the kitchen lay. Not bothering to sit down as he had suggested, she placed her shoulder bag on a sofa before stepping out of her heels; walking right behind him. Aaradhya had a tough time not to let her drool soil the marble floor as her eyes clung to his taut butt. He probably had the sexiest butt she had ever seen. Not that she was in the habit of checking men's butts. But no woman could possibly ignore Advik's, for sure.

He turned around suddenly to catch her gaze lowered to study his figure, a smile tilting his lips at the corners when he noticed her blush. Good!

"I… er… I thought I'll help you with the coffee," she stammered, feeling a deep urge to fan herself when she noticed the flare of heat in his chocolatey gaze.

He shrugged. "Why not?" He didn't take his eyes off her as he added coffee powder to the electric filter before pouring water in its slot. Switching on the filter, he took some milk from the fridge to heat in a pan. Placing a couple of mugs on a tray, he opened the sugar jar to ask, "How much?" his voice gruff.

"Advik…"

Lifting a hand in front of him as if to ward her off, he said, "Do you take sugar in your coffee?" He had to ignore the expression on her face. Or he might simply succumb to both their overwhelming needs.

"Dump the whole jar in it, damn you!" Aaradhya snarled even as she glared at him. Who wanted to have some bloody coffee at this hour anyway?

"Aara?" Suddenly, he was standing way closer to her than he had meant to. Taking her slender shoulders in his hands, he ran his gaze over her flushed face, groaning when he saw her white teeth snagging her lush lower lip. "Don't!"

"Don't what?" she asked, looking up into his face, studying him with equal interest.

"I thought you understood," he said, his voice a whisper as he watched his own hand in morbid fascination. It seemed to have a life of its own as it left her shoulder to cup her cheek, a thumb tracing the shape slowly and deliciously. Her skin was softer than a rose petal, he noted, his eyes open in a half slit as he wondered if he would ever regain control over his hand.

Turning her head, she kissed his caressing hand, her gaze clinging to his. "What?"

"Aara…" He gave a groan of protest even as the nerve ends on his palm came alive, shooting electrical sparks throughout his body, making him go hard with yearning. "Listen, I explained to you that I don't really have time for a…" He stopped when he heard a hiss. "Shit!" He let go of her to rush to the gas stove before switching it off, the milk having boiled over. Taking a couple of deep, shuddering breaths to bring his libido under control—or at least he tried—he switched off the coffee filter before pouring the coffee and milk into the mugs. He added sugar to both, not bothering to ask her again about her preference. What did it matter? She could add more of everything in case it wasn't to her taste. Placing two spoons on the tray, he carried it to the living room, turning to call over his shoulder, "Let's go sit in the hall."

Gritting her teeth in frustration, Aaradhya followed Advik, her gaze fixed on his shoulder blades. *No, I will NOT look at his butt, not again.*

"I hope you like your coffee," he said, trying to be polite. All he wanted to do was to lift her in his arms and carry her off to his bedroom. Smothering the groan that tried to erupt from his throat, he glared at her as if it was all her fault.

"I don't give a damn. Tell me something, Advik. Is it really coffee that you want just now?" she challenged, a shapely eyebrow up in query as she looked deeply into his eyes.

"Damn it, Aara. You know what I want!" Crossing his arms across his chest, he turned away to walk to the floor length windows, his body taut with longing. His manhood was so hard that it was all set to burst forth from the confines of his jeans.

"So what's stopping you?" she asked, sliding her arms around his lean waist and leaning against his broad back. It felt so heavenly, pressing her heated body against his hard, muscled back, her hips fitting snugly against his lean thighs.

"Aara!" Advik jumped before turning swiftly to push her away, his hands hard on her arms. She would have fallen down if he hadn't held her. "Are you crazy?"

She bit her lip to stop herself from smiling when she saw the colour high on his lean cheeks. It was obvious that he wanted her as much as she wanted him. "I suppose I am," she said in a soft voice, shutting one eye in a wink.

"Aara…" He removed his hands from her arms to take a few steps away, shaking his head. "I can see that you are."

"Advik, listen. I understand that you are a busy man and don't have time for a relationship. But right now, you are here; I am here. I don't think either of us is going to get much sleep, not in the aroused state we both are in. Why not make us both happy by giving in to temptation?"

She was Temptation with a capital T, definitely. He couldn't deny that. That she was bold it had been obvious right from the first time he met her. But he couldn't believe that she was keen on a one-night stand. Nor did he believe that he was going to be satisfied with spending just one night in her arms.

Why the hell did I go and invite her to dinner? Should have left well alone.

Advik walked to the sofa and plopped down. Taking a mug in his hand, he quickly sipped on the coffee. "Why don't you have your coffee before it grows cold?" he invited.

She plunked down right next to him on the sofa before taking a coffee mug in a slender hand. Her gaze accusing as she pouted at him, she sipped on the coffee before automatically shutting her eyes. "Mmm… this is delicious," she moaned, drinking the coffee greedily.

Did she have to be so damn sensuous while drinking coffee of all things in the world? Advik wanted to protest, his body responding to every nuance in her expression. He kept his empty coffee mug on the tray with a loud thud before jumping to his feet. She was sitting too damn close to him for comfort.

Does he really think he can escape me—what we feel for each other—forever? Aaradhya placed her empty mug on the tray before getting up too. Lifting the tray in her hand, she carried it to the kitchen.

"You don't have to do the washing, Aara. My maid will come in the morning to clean everything up."

Actually, he couldn't wait to get rid of his late-night guest. Or he might simply go mad. That he was going to spend a sleepless night was a foregone conclusion, of course.

"Okay," she called out, placing the tray next to the sink in the kitchen before stepping back into the hall. Her hands on her hips, she went to stand in front of him. "Are you at least going to kiss me goodbye, or no?" she asked, pinning him with her sharp gaze.

"Won't your parents be worried about you? It's past one," he said in the way of reply.

"I don't live with my parents."

His imagination running crazily about her single life, he asked, "You live alone?"

"Not really. What is this we are playing at? Twenty questions?" she asked, her voice mildly sarcastic.

Not really bothered by her sarcasm, he asked, "What does that mean? You either live alone or you don't. I…"

"I live with my grandparents."

He whistled. "Don't they mind if you stay out so late?"

She shrugged. "They know I'm a big girl now. After all, I've been living abroad, all by myself, for almost two years." This time, the sarcasm was even more obvious than before.

What does he have running in his veins? Ice?

"Are you gay, Advik?" she asked outright. Somehow, she was confident he wasn't, not the way he reacted to her proximity.

"What????" Advik glared at her even as she stepped closer to him. "Of course not."

"I didn't think so, either," she said in a mischievous whisper, her eyes dancing as they clung to his. Tracing a finger over the shape of his moustache from one end to the other, she went on her tiptoes to press her mouth to his. When she felt him shudder against her body, she responded by tracing the tip of her tongue over the shape of his lips. "Advik…"

With a loud groan, Advik gathered her in his arms, opening his mouth to capture her lips in a torrid kiss, his tongue mating with her enthusiastic one. Time came to a standstill in the living room of his flat as they kissed deeply, again and again, coming up for some air every few minutes before getting back to the task at hand. Her arms were locked tightly around his neck, while his caressed her bare waist after pushing her t-shirt out of the way.

It was a long time before Advik buried his face in the crook of her shoulder, breathing deeply in of her feminine scent that was citrusy and all things woman. He took deep and steadying breaths, trying to get a control of his libido, but without much success.

As for Aaradhya, she rubbed her cheek against his chest, feeling his heat despite the t-shirt he was still wearing. If she had her way, it would have been off him. But it was obvious that he wasn't going to make love to her fully, at least not tonight. While her body clamoured for mating with him, she supposed she could wait a bit longer. Removing her arms from around his neck, she brought them around his waist, pulling his t-shirt out of the waistband of his jeans to run her hands over his bare back. Oh my God! It was like touching steel encased in velvet. Her hands roamed freely as she caressed his back, waist up.

"Stop it, Aara." It was an effort for Advik to pull out of her arms to stand a couple of feet away.

"You don't like my touch?" she asked, fluttering her eyelashes at him, a knowing smile on her face.

"I think you should go home," he said, walking away to the doorway to get her shoes. "Here, put these on."

She plopped down on the sofa and leaned back. "Do you want to do it for me?" she asked, glancing at him challengingly.

Catching the upward thrust of her breasts, Advik shut his eyes for a moment, only to open them in a hurry as his imagination ran riot. Not uttering a word, he went down on his knees to help her into her shoes. It was an erotic experience, touching her bare feet as he slid her shoes on, one by one. His jaw tight with tension, he completed the task, refusing to glance at her face. Once done, he got up to stand. Taking her hand in his, he pulled her from the sofa before dragging her over to the door.

"Good bye!"

Aaradhya walked back to the sofa and took her shoulder bag. "I'll see you then."

"Or maybe not," he responded, shutting the door firmly in her face.

Coward! he called himself. That he didn't sleep a wink that night was no one's fault but his own.

10

Hey, what's up?

Advik opened the chat box on his Tinder app to look at Aaradhya's message the next morning. It had come at three, soon after she reached home, he presumed. Oh boy, was he tempted to tell her what was literally up! He refrained from doing so, but it was an effort. He felt so drawn to her, just like a bee to a honeypot. It was a wonder that he had resisted making love to her last night, despite his clamouring body.

But there lay the difference. If it had been in the US or UK, he would have accepted his date's obvious invitation. He wouldn't be expected to marry the woman. But it was so different in India. Aaradhya might have lived abroad for a few years, but that didn't mean she would have forgotten her Indian roots. He didn't think she would be open to a one-night stand, which is all he could offer her at this point in his life.

And what if someone from her family, her father or even her grandfather whom she lived with, came after him with a stick or maybe even a gun, insisting that he wed her? Advik shuddered, his imagination running wild. But again, he couldn't deny the fact that he had been tempted… so damn tempted that he still couldn't remember how he had resisted.

Her lovely face, her soft skin, the heat in her gaze and her sizzling touch had driven him crazy. As for the kisses they had shared, they had set his blood soaring, his whole body going taut with need, especially his manhood. It had throbbed so hungrily, driving him with the need to bury itself within her core.

God damn it all!

He jumped to his feet, throwing his phone on the sofa. *No, I'm not going to reply.* Or they will get to chatting more and more, and soon he would find himself agreeing to meet her again. No way was he going to do that, not in the near future, if ever.

It was almost ten in the morning when Aaradhya woke up, stretching luxuriously, a wide smile on her face. Last night had been fun. Yes, she had found it difficult to go to sleep as she craved to be in Advik's arms; keen to make love with him. But well, she had tried. And he had resisted.

Her smile stretched into a grin. She knew for a fact that he had been right at the edge, ready to give in to their pent-up desire at any moment. Only she had stopped pushing after a point. After all, if he truly desired her, he wouldn't need to be pushed, would he?

She gurgled with laughter as she got up to go to the bathroom, removing her nightshirt before stepping under the shower. Advik was fun to be with, the conversation flowing back and forth easily, jumping to any number of subjects. Though, every time, it got back to a common favourite—food.

And he was too damn pleasing to the eye. Like, she couldn't take her gaze off him throughout the time they had spent together. And every time they got within a few inches of each other, the whole air appeared to sizzle around them, the energy inching to a different level altogether.

She had enjoyed touching him, and had loved it when his large, masculine hands had caressed the bare skin of her waist. And the kisses had been mind-blowing. So much so that she already hungered for them first thing this morning.

Humming a tune, Aaradhya stepped out of the bathroom to throw open her wardrobe. Running a hand down the clothes hanging there, she pulled out a halter neck dress that barely touched her knees. Well, her grandmother might not approve, but so what? Savitri wouldn't dream of telling her granddaughter to change out of the outfit.

Today, everything Aaradhya did was with Advik in mind. She couldn't help wondering what he would think, say, if he saw her in this dress which was a sunny yellow colour with white trimming. Brushing her hair thoroughly, she gathered its length up in a high pony with a white scrunchy. Thrusting her feet into the rubber sandals that she wore at home, she went out of her room and directly into the kitchen.

"Hello, *Paati*, good morning!" Aaradhya hugged her grandmother before kissing her on her plump cheek.

"Good morning, good morning. You are late, Aara," said Savitri, stirring the *sambar* with a stainless-steel ladle, as it boiled in a *kal chetti*—stoneware typically used in South Indian kitchens in yonder days—that she had placed on the gas stove.

"Something smells so awesome, *Paati,*" said Aaradhya, quickly changing the subject. Savitri was used to waking up at five in the morning, followed by Ramani who also woke up around that time. Aaradhya got up whenever she pleased, never following a time table. Being the youngest in the family and the only girl in her generation, she was the apple of her grandfather's eye and rather spoilt in her ways. But not so much that she behaved badly.

Savitri turned to gaze at the young woman, a small scowl puckering her eyebrows when she noticed her attire. Not bothering to comment on it, she said, "I'm making *sambar* with multiple vegetables; along with freshly ground *sambar masala.*"

"Woohoo! My favourite. You are the best, *Paati*. I love you." She kissed her grandmother again before getting a *dabara* and *tumbler* to mix herself some filter coffee.

"Here, let me get that for you. In fact, your *Thatha* and I will join you as we are ready for a second dose."

"Perfect," said Aaradhya, pulling out a draw to remove a tray before placing three sets of *dabara tumbler* on it while Savitri mixed the filter coffee decoction, boiling milk and sugar in a vessel before pouring it into the tumblers. Both grandmother and granddaughter went into the living room in search of Ramani.

"*Enna,* why don't you join us for coffee?" Savitri called out to her husband who was reading The Times of India from one end to the other.

"Good morning, *Thatha,*" called out Aaradhya cheerfully, kissing her grandfather on a wrinkled cheek.

"Good morning, Aara. You're looking nice. Are you planning to go out?" he asked, pulling her down next to him on the sofa.

"I'm thinking. I've no baking to do today. I…"

Sipping his coffee, Ramani gave his grandchild a shrewd glance. "Were you out late last night?"

Savitri sat up straighter to stare at her granddaughter. She hadn't known about it.

Aaradhya looked from one grandparent to the other and back again, with a naughty smile, same as that of a small child caught stealing from a cookie jar. "Hmm…" she said, closing her eyes as she relished her coffee. "This is so yum, *Paati.*" She was getting really adept at changing the subject, it seemed.

"Aara?" said Ramani, pinning her with his dark gaze. "You haven't answered my question."

"Yes, *Thatha*. I was out for dinner with a friend."

"Till two am?" He was persistent.

She shrugged. "I'm still getting used to our time zone after living abroad for so long, *Thatha*. I hope you don't mind?"

He looked her up and down, not saying anything. Ramani was clear that he wanted his grandchild to have all the freedom she wanted. But that didn't stop him from being a mite worried when she stayed out ıte at nights. Anyway, he had too much faith in the almighty and didn't really believe that she would come to any harm. He reached forward to pat her shoulder. "No worries, my child."

Savitri didn't pass any comment as she listened to their conversation. There was a time when she had believed that she knew best. But after seeing the way her daughter, Janani, had chosen to remain a spinster just because she couldn't wed the man she loved, the matriarch had realised that people weren't all the same; they had different thoughts and beliefs, even if they belonged to the same family. It had taken her many years to understand the depth of her daughter's love for Kartik Hegde. That Kartik was the son of the woman Savitri hated from the depth of her heart was another matter. That his mother was the snooty Akshatha Hegde who thought no end of herself was something which did not really matter to the youngsters. Both of them, Kartik and Janani, had chosen to remain single and Savitri's heart went out to them. It was only after the fall out had Savitri realised the real meaning of frustration and the complete lack of control over a situation.

It had taken barely fifteen minutes and some really hurtful words for Savitri and Akshatha to tear apart the friendship between their respective husbands; one which had lasted for more than a quarter century. Even today, despite her husband having forgiven her, Savitri regretted the role she had played in the drama that evening when she and Ramani had gone to meet the Hegdes to ask for Kartik's hand for Janani.

Sigh!

Janani had accepted her single existence. But the mother couldn't forgive herself for the same.

Aaradhya took the tray with the empty coffee containers and walked back to the kitchen along with her grandmother. "When do you think brunch will be ready, *Paati*?" she asked.

"In about half an hour or so. Are you hungry?"

Aaradhya shook her head. "Not all that hungry. But I'm planning to go out for the rest of the day."

"Alright. We will all eat soon."

"Can I help you with something, *Paati*?" asked Aaradhya.

"No, my child. Ramu has already cut all the vegetables. I will just have to cook them. You go on and do whatever you need to do. I will call you when the food is ready."

"Okay, *Paati*," said Aaradhya, walking out of the kitchen.

Savitri adored her granddaughter. And she was the first one to admit how hard Aaradhya worked. She definitely deserved the break. She switched on the stove and turned her attention to making brunch.

In the Hegde household, it was only Akshatha and her younger son Kartik for lunch that afternoon. The Hegde matriarch looked at her silent son as he nibbled at the food on his plate, an inadvertent sigh bursting forth from her.

"Don't you like the food?"

"Huh!" Kartik looked up at his mother as if he had just noticed that she was sitting next to him at the dining table. "What?"

"Don't you like the food?" she repeated the question, doing her best to curb her rising irritation.

Kartik shrugged. "What's there not to like? It's *bisi bele bath* and *brinjal fry*. Not bad, I suppose."

"There is also your favourite *tomato rasam*. And I asked the cook to make *green tomato chutney* all because you are having lunch at home after so long." She pushed the bowl of the spicy chutney towards him.

Akshatha tried hard to get close to her younger son. But she could see that it was impossible. There was a time when her son had truly loved and respected her. But not for such a long time now. Kartik had never forgiven her for stopping his alliance with the Iyer girl. Stupid boy! He didn't understand that the Iyers were nowhere near as rich as the Hegdes. The girl would have never fitted into their household. What Akshatha had not expected was for her son to remain a bachelor all these years. And where had the years gone? He was all of forty-five now.

Without responding to his mother's words, Kartik served some *rasam* in a glass cup and drank from it. He also spooned some of the spicy chutney onto his plate and continued to eat silently.

"How is Advik?" asked Akshatha, eating from her plate, though her eyes were studying her son.

"Why ask me? Don't you know?" he asked, lifting his gaze to her face even as a quick anger surfaced in him.

"How will I know?" she asked, a bewildered expression on her face. "Who tells me anything in this house?"

"Oh really, *Amma*? Don't you have your grandson's phone number? He's been back in Mumbai for so long and you haven't even bothered to speak to him." Kartik glared at his mother. "And don't give me the bullshit that he hasn't called you. I know differently."

"Kartik…" Akshatha placed a pacifying hand over his as it lay on the dining table beside his plate. "You know how your father is. He didn't want Advik to come into the house. And he refuses to speak to him. How can I cross my husband and be in touch with the boy? Tell me."

Kartik pushed back his chair noisily as he jumped to his feet, the food on his plate only half eaten. "You must be joking, *Amma*. Don't tell me that you take your husband's permission every time you do something. That must be the biggest joke on this earth." Sparks flew from his brown gaze as he scowled deeply at his mother.

At seventy, Akshatha was twelve years younger than her husband; and maintained excellent health. She was extremely particular about what she ate, how much she ate and made it a point to practise yoga and meditation all seven days of the week. Despite all that, she was anything but peaceful at heart. In spite of all the wealth and property which she owned, not just from her parents', but also from her husband, she was an unhappy woman. She also felt jealous of every woman her age; especially of Savitri Iyer.

Savitri was from a poor family and her parents had not paid one paisa as dowry when she married Ramani Iyer. Even the diamond earrings that she possessed had been given to her by her husband. Akshatha had been terribly shocked when she had got to know about all this through her husband. Bhaskar Hegde, who was such an intelligent business man, had become his young and beautiful wife Akshatha's puppet after their marriage. He hadn't really bothered to know her nature fully before sharing every little incident from his past. It had never struck him that he was making a mistake in confessing everything to his wife, unaware that the proud and arrogant Akshatha had found many reasons to not just dislike Savitri, but even hate her. After all, how could the young bride swallow the fact that her new husband had a high regard not only for his partner, but also his partner's wife, Savitri?

Throughout the time the partnership had continued despite Akshatha doing her best to throw a spanner in the works from time to time, she had schemed and she had schemed some more. Finally, the opportunity had presented itself when Ramani Iyer and his wife came to their home, begging for a marriage between their foolish daughter and the Hegdes' younger son. As if she would have ever agreed to the match! Her Kartik was so handsome and intelligent. Whereas, that Janani was so thin and pale. And she was an artist over all that. What kind of a job was it, being an artist? And why did a woman need to work at all? Which must be because the Iyers were poor. Akshatha conveniently forgot the fact that Bhaskar Hegde and Ramani Iyer were equal partners. If Bhaskar brought home a profit of more than one lakh rupees in a month, then Ramani also must be taking home an equal amount. Didn't that make the Iyers rich too?

Akshatha wasn't very logical by nature. She felt she was too much of an aristocrat to let Savitri become her *sambandhi*. No way!

Even now, with Kartik spending his life as a bachelor, his mother didn't think it was her fault. How could it be? She had only objected to Janani becoming her son's wife. He could have chosen just about any other young lady from their community. In fact, she had even tried to introduce him to a number of them, all carefully selected from rich families. But the boy had simply refused to budge from his stand. He had told both his parents categorically that he would never get married.

And now, this Advik, her only grandson who was just twenty-eight years old, had dared to defy his grandparents. Where was the need to go to America to study? What was there that wasn't here in India? And look at him, after roaming all over the world, he was back in Mumbai and wanted to become a part of the family business. She couldn't blame her husband for refusing to allow the boy back into their home. Why should they? Had he listened to them before going abroad?

Total waste of money!

And look at Kartik now. He was accusing her of not getting in touch with her grandson. How dare he?!

"Listen Kartik," she said firmly. "If I had thought your father was wrong in refusing Advik entry in our home, I would have definitely told him so. But I agree with him in this matter. Advik shouldn't have gone away like that. Especially when his grandfather told him not to. What is there to learn from there? Whatever Advik needs to know, he has already learned from your *Appa*. He could have simply joined Mysuru Ahara along with you and Ganesh. He would have become a millionaire by now. He..."

"Really? If that were the case, I should be a millionaire many times over, right? Why don't I have more than fifty thousand rupees in my bank account?" asked Kartik angrily.

Akshatha shrugged. "I wasn't speaking about you. We were discussing about Advik just now..."

"How could Advik become a millionaire in four years when I don't have even one lakh after working for *Appa* in thirty years?" Kartik spoke in a low voice even though he wanted to shout at his mother. He held his temper in check knowing how stubborn she could be.

"That's because Advik is too clever by half. He insisted on taking a salary right from day one. Which neither you nor your brother bothered to ask your father."

"You mean *Appa* would have given us salaries if we had asked?" Kartik couldn't believe what he was hearing. Had he and Ganesh been really stupid not demanding for a monthly sum? After all, they had spent their whole lives slogging away at the family restaurant; following every diktat of the old man's.

"Well, I'm not so sure about that. But you can't deny that your father did pay Advik a salary when he demanded. Maybe..."

Kartik raised his hand to stop his mother from speaking further, thoroughly disgusted to hear her words. It was all a sham! Both his parents—yes, even his mother—were control freaks. And he had to agree with his mother about Advik. He had been smart enough not just to demand a monthly salary, but had managed to save the whole amount over a period. Which was how he had gotten away from under the Hegde patriarch's thumb.

His nephew was smart indeed!

11

It was a few minutes before eleven pm when Aaradhya waited outside the Italian joint at Palladium Mall, watching the last trickle of customers come and go. She had been waiting for fifteen minutes, determined to catch Advik when he stepped out of his work place. It was obvious to her that he wasn't keen on meeting her again, though she couldn't really see why. It was too obvious that he was attracted to her as much as she was enamoured by him.

How to make him understand that she had no expectations from him? They both liked each other and the chemistry was nothing short of mind-blowing. Why not enjoy each other's company whenever possible?

And Aaradhya wasn't one to wait for him to take the step forward. If he needed a push in the right direction, she was only too ready to give it, she thought to herself, a smile on her face. She stood up straight when she noticed the very man she had been thinking about, walk out of the restaurant.

"Hey!" She stepped forward to snag his arm.

Advik's head whipped around, his face going pale with shock when he saw the woman who haunted not just his dreams, but all his waking moments too, standing in front of him, looking absolutely gorgeous and smiling at him so brilliantly. A part of him wished that she had simply remained a contact on the Tinder app. While another part rejoiced to see her standing right there in front of him.

"Hey!" His voice was gruff when he returned her greeting. Clearing his throat, he asked, "What are you doing here?"

"Isn't it obvious?" she asked, her smile widening into a grin. "I'm here to meet you. Wanna go for a drink at The Irish House?"

Oh, he was tempted! And how! All the lectures he had read himself through the sleepless night went out of the window on seeing her in person.

"Come on, Advik, say yes," she persuaded, scrunching her nose at him.

Cute! And, oh so kissable! Yes, even her nose. He gave her a nod before walking along with her. She took his hand in hers, locking her fingers loosely with his, her soft palm pressing against his hard one.

Advik was a goner! He realised that there was only so much he could resist. Her gentle touch brought to life every single nerve in his hand, making the blood race through his veins, stoking the fire deeply within him, one which was already burning bright for her.

Sensing his capitulation, she leaned her head on his shoulder as they walked across to Phoenix Mall before taking the escalator to The Irish House. She gave a soft sigh of happiness when he let go of her hand to wrap his arm around her slender waist before pulling her closer.

The conversation was non-existent as they looked into each other's eyes while guzzling from a pint of beer each. It was obvious that neither was keen on the drink even before the waiter had brought it to them.

"Have you brought your car?" he asked, his voice almost a whisper.

"Hmm."

"Let's go." He placed the bill amount and a generous tip on the table before taking her hand in his and pulling her out of the pub.

She didn't deny him when he asked for the car keys before driving them out of the parking area as if his tail was on fire. It was obvious that he wanted to get home as quickly as possible.

They reached his building in record time. Glad that there was no one to accompany them in the elevator, Advik pulled her roughly into his arms before kissing her deeply, his tongue mating with hers erotically.

"Mmm…" She protested when he lifted his head to grin down at her.

"What? Do you want to do this in the lift?" he asked, his dimples flashing even as his eyes crinkled at the corners.

"Do you know how hot you look when you actually smile? Especially with your eyes?" she asked, an expression of wonder on her face.

He threw back his head and laughed, lifting her into his arms when he realised that she wasn't going to do much other than stare at his face.

"What's so funny?" she asked, giving him a mock glare, her forearms braced on his muscular shoulders, relishing the feel of his arms locked behind her thighs.

"You!"

"I object," she protested, stepping out of his hold when he let her slide down to the floor right outside his door.

"To what?" he asked, an eyebrow up as he placed the key in the lock and opened the door.

"You laughing at me," she pouted.

Turning around to wrap his right arm around her, he pulled her against his tautly aroused body even as he shut the door closed with his left hand. "I wasn't laughing *at* you, Aara." Pressing his forehead to hers, he looked deeply into her eyes. "I was just laughing with joy. Thank you for coming over to meet me today."

She shook her head at him, her hands pressed to his chest, where his heart thudded heavily. Meeting his heated gaze, she licked her suddenly dry lips. "You wouldn't have bothered to call me otherwise, right?" Her gaze turned accusing.

He gave a shuddering sigh, his hands working their way lower to cup her shapely buttocks before pulling her close to his throbbing manhood. "You, my Aara, are too damn desirable. I've been having the devil's own time resisting you. And you know that, don't you?"

It was her turn to laugh mischievously. "Oh yes! Or I wouldn't have dared to chase you."

"Aara…" He buried his face in the crook of her shoulder, breathing deeply of her feminine scent before opening his mouth to kiss the rapid pulse beating there. Highly aroused when he felt the pulse rate picking up, he reached out to stroke it with the tip of his tongue, making her moan in delight.

Aaradhya wrapped her arms tightly around his lean waist, pulling his t-shirt out of the waistband of his jeans to explore the rippling muscles of his back. Even as she caressed him, she was completely aware of his erection throbbing against her abdomen. She pressed her lower body closer to his and was thrilled to hear his groan of need.

Speaking into her ear, he said, "Aara… babe, I want you to understand that I can't offer you anything long term. I…"

She drew back to place a hand over his mouth, shutting him up effectively. "Shall we take it one day at a time? Just now, I desperately want you inside me. Please Advik… can we move on to your bedroom?" She fluttered her eyelashes at him for good measure.

He took her pleading lips in his, kissing her deeply, again and again. Lifting her up in his arms once again, he carried her to his bedroom.

He looked into her eyes as he untied the knot of her halter dress. "You look so damn sexy in this dress," he said, pulling the strings down slowly.

"Believe me, I look even sexier out of it," she flirted, giving him a saucy grin.

He laughed, unable to stop himself, before choking up when the dress fell down to her waist. She was wearing no bra within and he couldn't help staring at her plump, rounded breasts. "Gorgeous," he whispered, reaching a thumb to touch one of the tips, fascinated when it puckered under his caress.

"Advik…" She leaned into his touch, revelling in it when he cupped a large hand over the breast, her head falling back on his shoulder. "It feels so good…"

He let go of her, grinning at her protest even as he pulled his t-shirt off, laughing when he saw the way her eyes went wide as her gaze fell on his wide chest.

"Wow! You are so damn fit," she said, running both her hands over his naked chest, revelling in the texture of short, crisp curls spread over all that hard muscle. Leaning forward, she kissed a flat nipple before stroking it with her tongue.

Advik moaned long and hard, wrapping his arms tightly around her before caressing her back. "I like your tongue on me, babe."

She worked her way across his chest to caress the other nipple, taking a gentle bite of it, laughing when she heard his growl. "You taste damn good, you know."

Pushing her dress down her legs, he backed her on to the bed before lying down next to her, his hands cupping her breasts, her pebbled nipples pressing against his palms. He rubbed his face against them, revelling in the whimpers emanating from her throat. Turning his head, he stroked the tip of her breast with his tongue before drawing it into his mouth, making her gasp with pleasure.

Aaradhya tunnelled her fingers through his hair, pulling his head close to her body, her legs thrashing as he suckled deeply of her breast. She felt pressure build up in her womb when he turned to give her other breast his attention, her legs thrashing some more on the bed. She ran her restless hands over his back, the tactile sensation vying with the rapture she felt as he feasted on her breasts.

Advik took her left hand and lifted it up to press it down on the pillow next to her head, his fingers locking with hers. The gesture brought her upper body closer to him as he continued to worship her breasts. He took her right hand and placed it against his tumescent penis, smiling when he felt her gentle and hesitant touch.

But Aaradhya being what she was, she lost her hesitation almost immediately, her hand caressing him firmly down the length, her thumb rubbing over the tip in a circle, again and again.

"Awww, babe. That feels so good," he groaned, rising up to kiss her on her eager lips, his tongue pushing into her mouth hungrily. He stopped kissing her to lift his head to look down at her, the muscles straining on his shoulders as he fought for control when a sudden thought struck him. "Are you a virgin?"

"Huh?" Her hand stopped midway in its caress as Aaradhya stared at him, a confused expression on her face. "Why? Are you?" she asked, the confusion turning into curiosity.

"Very funny," he chuckled weakly. "Of course I am not. I am asking you, only because I don't want to hurt you."

She shrugged, her bouncing breasts drawing his heated gaze. "I'm not either."

Phew! He bent down to love her breasts some more before kissing his way down her abdomen, smiling when he felt her quiver under his touch as he tickled her skin with his luxuriant moustache. Dipping his tongue into her navel, he lifted his gaze to hers, a cocky eyebrow up in query.

"You're too far away," she grumbled, her hands tugging at his hair as she tried to pull him up.

His laughter brushed over her sensitive skin, making her shiver some more. "I know. But I'm exactly where I want to be," he declared, his hands running over her slim thighs, parting her legs wide and going on his knees, his eyes avidly studying her femininity.

"Advik…?" Aaradhya stared at him in fascination, watching him studying her body. She felt anything but shy; rather proud of the attraction she held for him. She gulped when she felt a large hand cup her vagina, gently running up and down over her curls. "Advik……"

"You like it?" he asked, his voice a whisper, his gaze still on her lower body.

"Too much," she responded with alacrity, her hands fisting over the bedspread.

He moved further down on the bed before reaching forward to replace his hand with his mouth, kissing the lips of her vulva. Lifting her legs, he draped them over his shoulders before drawing his tongue down the seam. "You taste too damn good, babe," he said, gently suckling on her core.

Aaradhya's body went taut with the onslaught of sensations, her lower body lifting up in the air as she pressed herself closer to his stroking tongue, revelling in it. She felt the pressure building in her womb all over again, way more than before when he had been fondling her breasts.

"Advik!" she shouted impatiently, "Please, I want you inside me, NOW."

He laughed, licking his lips before lifting himself up to lie against her. Reaching across to the bedside table, he opened his wallet to remove the foil packet, tore it with his teeth and pulled out a condom.

"Allow me," she said, sitting up to push him back on the bed. Holding the condom in one hand, she leaned forward to kiss him on his penis before closing her mouth over the tip. Wrapping a hand around his thickened manhood, she drew him deeply into her mouth, rubbing her tongue over the head, again and again.

"Aaraaaaaaa…" The laughter had disappeared from his face as he stared at her in fascination, adoring the sensation of her mouth on him. "No more, babe," he called out, sitting up on the bed. Tugging her hair with both his hands, he stopped her from making him come immediately.

"You don't like it?" she asked, her slumberous gaze fixed on his face even as a slow smile tugged at her lips. She knew for a fact that he had enjoyed it as much as she had, or maybe more. At least, his body had as it responded to her by growing bigger and harder.

"You know I love it. But I want to bury myself inside you," he said, pulling her close to speak into her ear, his teeth gently sinking into her earlobe as he took a bite, "Deep inside your core."

She turned her head to meet his lips with her own. "Yes, please." She reached across to take his pulsing manhood in her hands before drawing the condom over it. "There!" she said, giving him a naughty yank.

His eyes promised retribution as he pushed her back on the bed before going on his knees between her legs. Lifting her right leg to wrap it around his waist, he placed the tip of his penis at the entrance to her vagina, pushing gently within.

An impatient Aaradhya threw her left leg around his waist to lock it with her right ankle at the small of his back, thrusting upwards to meet him halfway.

He pushed deeply into her with a satisfied grunt before he was completely buried within her. "It feels so amazing to be sheathed in your warmth," he said, kissing her hungrily. It wasn't long before he pulled out of her to push back right within, setting the pace.

She met him thrust for thrust, her hands on his back, her nails digging into his flesh even as she pressed light kisses along his masculine jaw. The tips of her breasts revelled when they came up against his hard chest, enjoying the feel of hair brushing against her sensitive skin.

Sweat broke out on their skin as they made love, pulling and pushing as they reached out to the peak, groaning and moaning as one. Soon, the pressure that had been building inside Aaradhya reached its summit, breaking through in a volcano of sensation and reaching a climax, making her tremble in the aftermath for a long time to come. The ecstasy only doubled when he came soon after, his heaving body falling limply over hers.

"Give me a moment, babe. I can't move," he whispered apologetically, bothered about squashing her with his weight, not that he was in a state to do anything about it. It was a wonder that he could find his voice at all, not after that earth shaking orgasm, never before experienced in his life.

She wrapped her arms and legs around him, clinging to him like a limpet, refusing to let him go. "Goodnight," she whispered, shutting her eyes to fall asleep almost immediately.

Due to the combination of a sleepless night and some spectacular lovemaking, Advik also fell asleep, his face buried in her soft breasts.

Aaradhya came awake sometime later, only by instinct. She tried to stretch her limbs and smiled inadvertently when she felt them weighed down by a deliciously masculine form. Caressing his cheek with a hand, she kissed the top of Advik's head. "Move, lazybones. I need to go home."

His only response was a grunt before he turned on his side, spooning her back to his front; his hand firmly cupping her breast.

Laughing, Aaradhya wiggled out of his arms. "I have to go, Advik."

He opened his eyes halfway to give her a lazy glance. "What time is it?"

"Not two yet." She searched for her panties and pulled them on, her eyes drinking in his naked form.

"Come here," he said, turning on his back, his hands under his head. He raked her slender body with his gaze, smiling when he noticed her puckering nipples.

Unable to resist, she leaned over to kiss him fully on his mouth, quivering when she felt his hands on her breasts. "I think not, Advik. My grandfather notices if I go home very late."

"We don't need all that long. See what you do to me," he said, taking her hand and placing it on his rock-hard manhood.

Her eyes went wide when she felt him, her hand automatically curling around him in a caress. "That was quick," she said, her gaze locking with his.

"Hmm… mmm. My body craves you."

Grinning, she wiggled out of her panties to fall over him. Remembering just in time, she asked, "Do you have another condom?"

He reached across wordlessly to remove a second foil packet from his wallet to hand it over to her.

"You seem well prepared," she teased, her eyes rolling over when she felt his hands squeezing her breasts.

"What can I do? The way women throw themselves at me, I…"

"Meh!" She leaned across to take a bite of his lower lip before kissing him, effectively stopping him from speaking further.

Aaradhya left her naked lover half asleep in his bed, blowing him a kiss from the doorway before letting herself out of his apartment.

Advik smiled when he saw the message in his Tinder chat box the next morning.

Best sex I've ever had followed by several kissing emojis.

Wasn't it a good thing that he wasn't the blushing sort? Or Advik would have turned the shade of a beetroot.

Ditto he typed, pressing the enter button with a broad smile on his face.

12

Janani gave her niece a knowing smile. "Come on, spill it all," she invited. They were at Janani's home for their weekly lunch, a habit the two of them had formed over many years.

"Is it so obvious?" asked Aaradhya, her eyes shining with happiness when she thought of the time she had spent in Advik's arms.

"Maybe only to me. So, what's his name?"

"Advik."

"Just that? Does he have a surname?" Janani's eyes gleamed with mischief as she teased the younger woman.

A small frown puckered Aaradhya's smooth forehead as she thought long and hard before shaking her head slowly, a grin forming on her face. "I don't know."

Janani dramatically widened her eyes, placing both her hands one over the other on her mouth. "I can't believe this."

"Janani *Athai*, don't be so mean. I know it seems kind of strange, but I have met Advik a number of times..."

"…without even knowing his surname? Whoa! Don't mind me if I believe it all sounds pretty incredible to me."

Aaradhya gurgled with laughter. "Okay, I promise to find out the next time I meet him; which will probably be tonight." Soft colour ran up her cheeks when she met her aunt's curious gaze.

"Do you love him?" asked Janani.

"I think so. At least, I've never felt like this before. You know, a deep feeling of contentment when I am with him. Yeah, the lovemaking is amazing, but that's just a bonus. I just enjoy being with him. Do I sound cuckoo?"

The smile was wiped out from Janani's face as she stared at Aaradhya, her mind on the love of her own life. Shaking her head slowly, she said, "Not at all, my dear. You are pretty sound in mind. And yes, I am sure you are in love with your Advik."

Aaradhya gurgled with laughter. "He's not really my Advik, you know. He's not at all ready for commitment. Something about building his career and all that. I get the feeling that he wants to prove something, not just to himself, but to someone else as well." She shrugged. "I plan to take one day at a time. We meet when we both have time, which in itself is an effort. We chat on Tinder when we don't. What say?"

"I say that the present generation is the smartest." There was no bitterness in Janani's voice. But she couldn't stop the feeling of envy that crept in. How she wished she could have persuaded Kartik to be her lover even if they weren't married?! Except for the one time when he hadn't been able to say 'no' to her. But she never met him after that and it was definitely not due to lack of trying on her part. He had been adamant, believing that it would be insulting to Janani if he became her lover without the security of marriage. Damn him!

"Are you okay, *Athai*?" asked Aaradhya, noticing the lurking sadness at the back of her aunt's gaze.

Janani sighed, nodding. "Of course, I am."

Aaradhya quickly messaged Advik as she stepped out of her aunt's home soon after lunch.

Hey, what's your surname?

Hegde. And yours?

Iyer. It's funny how we never thought of finding out all this long.

Hehe.

She liked the fact that he replied almost instantaneously to her messages; unlike before when she had to wait for hours or even days to receive a response. Smiling, she typed out a message to her aunt on WhatsApp.

Advik's surname is Hegde.

Janani's instincts kicked in when she saw the message from Aaradhya. After all, how many Hegdes lived in Mumbai? She quickly typed into her WhatsApp window.

Is he from a hotelier family?

Don't know. Let me ask.

Aaradhya typed into the Tinder chat box.

Are you from a hotelier family?

Have you heard of Mysuru Ahara? In Matunga, not far from the railway station. My grandfather owns and runs it along with my father and uncle.

Oh! My granddad owns Madras Meals in the same area.

I can't believe this. Will talk more when we meet. Need to rush.

I'll see you tonight.

Not really understanding the depth of the enmity between the two families, Aaradhya typed with both her thumbs before pushing the send button on her message to her aunt. She hoped against hope that her aunt's wounds had healed by now as she sent her the message.

It's incredible that Advik's family—his grandpa, father and uncle—owns Mysuru Ahara. These are the same Hegdes who were Thatha's partners, I suppose. I've heard Paati mentioning a tiff and a fallout. I'm sure you know about it.

The colour drained out of Janani's face when she read her niece's message. Was this what they meant by history repeating itself? Her niece called it a tiff. The rift between the Iyers and Hegdes was more in the lines of a feud. And could be compared to none other than the Montagues and Capulets of William Shakespeare's tragedy, Romeo and Juliet.

Janani fell back on the sofa, her agenda for the afternoon forgotten as her thoughts insisted on travelling back down memory lane…

Janani couldn't believe her ears when her father called her over to his study and spoke to her about what had happened at Kartik's home that evening. It was only the earlier day when Janani had assured Kartik that her father would be able to persuade his to agree to a marriage between them.

But now, barely twenty-four hours later, her father was telling her that a marriage between Kartik and her was just not possible, not any more. Just as Kartik had said, his parents were completely against the match.

Ramani's face was pale with anxiety, his dark eyes appearing haunted as he held his daughter's hands in his. "My dear! I am truly sorry. I didn't mean to mess this up. I know how much you love Kartik and I also really like the boy. But..." He swallowed, doing his best to clear his choking throat, his eyes damp with unshed tears.

"*Appa...*" Janani turned paler still, seeing how upset her father was. "I don't understand, *Appa*. But, please, I don't really care if I marry Kartik or not; not if it's upsetting you so badly. Please don't cry, *Appa*. I cannot bear it." She jumped out of her chair to stand next to him, one hand on his shoulder as she used the other to wipe his face.

Ramani felt even more guilty, feeling that he had failed his favourite child. While it was no fault of his, that didn't stop him from feeling terrible about it. He shook his head sadly. "It's not just the alliance, Janu. My partnership with Bhaskar is also broken."

"What?" Janani's voice was a shocked whisper as she stared at her father, aghast. "Why? Because Kartik and I wanted to marry? Is it such a big sin, *Appa*?" She couldn't believe what she was hearing. She recalled

Kartik's despondency the earlier evening. He had been sure that his father was totally against a match between them. "I'm sorry, *Appa,*" she said, biting her lip to stop herself from crying out in pain. "I wish I had never told you about Kartik and asked you to fix our marriage."

"It's not your fault, my child. It's all fate. I think this dislike has been brewing for a long time. You must forgive your mother, Janu. Mrs Hegde has always treated Savitri like a lower being, all because she herself is from a richer family. And your mother has been putting up with all the insults for my sake. Today, the poison spewed out from both of them." He sighed, shaking his head once again. "There was so much of it, like it was enough to burn down our long partnership like the *halahala* poison from the ocean of milk itself." He quickly told her what had happened at the Hegde home, leaving out the colourful language used during the slanging match between the two women.

Janani stared at her father, unable to fully comprehend what he was saying. It appeared as if her mother Savitri had had an argument with Kartik's mother Akshatha; resulting in the end of the partnership between her father and his. Three decades of hard work and sweat! Gone down the drain in a flash. She couldn't believe what she was hearing.

What did it matter anyway? Her future appeared gloomy all of a sudden, one without Kartik in it. Because she knew for a fact that he would never agree to elope with her. She sighed. Well, she loved him for exactly what he was; not just portions of him that suited her. If he chose to live under his father's thumb, that's how Kartik was.

But that didn't mean she wouldn't try. With a determined thrust to her chin, Janani stood straight in front of her father. "*Appa,* you shouldn't worry on my account. I am your daughter and I have a strong spine. Even better is the fact that I have a beautiful career. There's more to life than marriage, I'm sure."

Ramani got up from his chair to place an arm around his daughter's shoulders, shaken more than ever when he felt her tremble within his hold. "My dear! God bless you!"

It took Janani more than a week to finally catch Kartik on the phone. Now that he had no workplace to go to—Madras Meals having come into Ramani Iyer's sole possession—the only place to contact him was at home. And it looked like everyone other than Kartik attended the calls at his house. When she finally heard his voice at the other end, she implored, "I want to meet you."

"What's the use?" he asked bitterly.

"I don't know. Will you meet me, or no?" she asked angrily.

"Okay."

"I'll pick you up near the flower shops at four."

"Okay," came the cheerless reply.

As Janani drove down the lane parallel to the flower shops, a small smile spread on her face when she saw Kartik standing in the corner. She stopped her car near him to lean across and open the passenger door.

Kartik quickly got inside to turn and look at her. "Are you sure you want to put us through this torture, Janu?" he asked.

Janani set the car in motion even as she studied him from her peripheral. There was a week's growth of beard on his face, and she was sure his hair had not seen a comb in a few days. He had also lost weight, with dark circles around his eyes. She shook her head at him. "Is it a torture to meet me?" she asked.

"You know it is. We can never belong to each other." His mouth drooped down at the corners as he glared at her.

"Come on, Kartik. We do belong to each other, whether we get married or not. As if a religious ceremony or court order is the only way to bind us! I don't know about you, but I belong to you, heart and soul," she declared vehemently, turning the car around King's Circle to take the opposite lane that led them to Don Bosco Church where she took a right again before driving straight.

He sighed, shutting his burning eyes to lean back in the seat. "You do know about me, Janu. I will never get married, not if I can't have you for my wife."

She smiled. "Which is what I wanted to know. Why don't we just run away?"

He sat up straight in his seat to look at her. "Are you crazy? I don't have a *paisa* to my name."

"Good. No one can accuse me of marrying you for your money," she grinned.

There was no answering smile on his face. "You *are* mad." He turned away to look straight, his arms crossed tightly against his chest.

They had reached Five Gardens by now and Janani parked the car across some street food carts. "That's true. I'm mad about you. Listen, Kartik. You can cook and you know how to do accounts. I can paint and my art already has a demand. My agent says it will only get bigger. We can plan to have a family after we make some money. Will it be so difficult?"

He shook his head vehemently. While Janani had had a life full of freedom, always having been encouraged to make her own decisions, Kartik had led a sheltered life, invariably having listened to what his father and mother said. While both Bhaskar and Akshatha had strong personalities, they had never allowed the same to develop in their children. Both their sons, Ganesh and Kartik, were good at following orders, but not taking decisions.

While he could understand that Janani's idea was definitely a good one, Kartik didn't have the guts to take action on it.

"This sounds good when we talk, Janu. But I don't think it will work on a practical basis."

Janani looked at his dear face, his square chin thrust out stubbornly. She didn't know if she should kiss him or shake him up. "Kartik…" She reached over to take his hand in hers. "I love you, Kartik. And I want to become yours."

He turned his burning gaze to look into her deep, dark one, his heart thudding with passion and desire.

"I'm sorry, Janu. I truly am." He valiantly controlled the tears that filmed over his eyes, from falling down his cheeks. "But I'm just not made up for living in penury. And I can't see you working your fingers to the bone. We both are used to luxurious lives. Please don't ask me to do it."

She placed a hand over his moving lips, shaking her head. "Okay, I'll accept that. But I want you to make love to me. One night! Please give me one night in your arms."

How could he refuse such a plea from the woman he not only loved, but desired to the point of madness?!

Janani wouldn't let them use protection. She hoped against hope that she would get pregnant during their union. But alas! It wasn't to be. She cursed the Gods when she got her periods barely a couple of weeks after they made love.

And that was it! The romance between Kartik and herself. It had been as ephemeral as raindrops on the desert ground.

Janani sat up with a start when she heard her phone ring…

She stared disbelievingly when she saw Kartik's face on the screen. She had managed to get his mobile number a few years ago, saving it to her phone. While she had never called him, it still felt wonderful to have a contact number. As for his picture, she had clicked it from an old picture from a family album.

"Hello, this is a surprise."

"Can we meet?"

It was a wonder that Janani managed not to faint when she heard those words in that gruff voice. "Kartik…?"

"Don't you want to?" he asked, a challenge in his voice.

"Of course I do. Do you want to come over to my flat? There's no one here."

"Are you sure your father wouldn't shoot me?"

She laughed out loud, her heart taking wings as it soared high. "If he does, I'll surely come to your rescue," she offered teasingly.

"Then yes, I'll come over."

"I live…"

"I always knew where you lived, Janu," he said.

"And it took you all this long…" Her voice turned hoarse with emotion.

"What to do, my love? You have chosen a coward for your boyfriend. I…"

"Shut up. And come over."

But Kartik never came while she waited and she waited; just as she had been waiting for the past twenty-three years.

Janani opened her eyes suddenly, touching her face to find it wet with tears. She had gone to sleep on the sofa while thinking about the past. And had dreamt of Kartik calling her on her cell.

Tch! Her life was one long dream, it seemed.

Advik couldn't wait for his lunch break. He so needed to speak to his father. No, it would be better to talk to Kartik Uncle. He had heard the story of his uncle being in love with someone from the Iyer family which owned Madras Meals. In fact, Advik recalled that that particular brand had been jointly owned by his grandfather, Bhaskar Hegde and his partner, Ramani Iyer. It was obvious to him by now that Aaradhya was a descendent of the same Ramani Iyer. The man was probably the grandfather she kept mentioning, the one she lived with.

Who had Kartik Uncle been in love with? He still held a candle to that woman, actually. Or he wouldn't remain a bachelor for all this long.

"Hello, Kartik *Chitthaiya*. Are you terribly busy?" asked Advik on the phone. He had chosen to have his lunch in his office cabin that afternoon.

"Never for you, brat. Go on, tell me," invited Kartik, lifting a hand to hail Dayaram to the accounting bay. Excusing himself, he stepped outside into the side lane to conduct the conversation with his nephew in peace.

"What do you know about Madras Meals? I mean the owners."

Kartik blanched. While it was true that the Iyers' restaurant wasn't all that far from theirs, he had somehow managed to ignore it, always turning his face away whenever he crossed the entry way. It was a good thing that Janani rarely visited the portals, or that's what he liked to believe. After all, he had never set eyes on her after the night they had spent together. It had broken his heart to a million pieces, letting go of the love of his life, but he hadn't really had a choice, had he? Clearing his throat now, he asked, "Why do you ask?"

Suddenly realising that he was probably stirring a hornets' nest, Advik backtracked. Maybe it was best not to talk about it over the phone. "Er... would you like to come over for a cup of coffee in the evening?" he asked his uncle.

"Where?" asked Kartik, a scowl on his face. What was his nephew getting at? "But wait, if it's to do with the Iyers, I would rather not."

"Not even if my girlfriend belonged to their family?" asked Advik, unaware of the impact of his words on his favourite uncle's blood pressure.

"What?" Kartik stopped in his tracks to yell into the phone. "What did you say?" He tried his best to bring down the decibel level, only to fail miserably.

"You heard me. I need to rush, *Chitthaiya*. Will you come over for coffee? I have a half an hour's break before the dinner crowd will begin to trickle in. 5.30?"

"Where?" Kartik's voice was a hoarse whisper.

"The Oriental Bowl at Inorbit Mall."

"You get coffee there?" asked Kartik, a sliver of a smile returning to his pale face as he joked.

"Yes, in my office. Will you come?"

"Try and stop me."

13

Unlike his nephew, Kartik knew everything there was to know about the Iyer family. He was aware of how successful Janani was in her career as an artist; how her paintings got sold even before they were completed. He knew that her brothers Chandar and Kumar were married and had children. Chandar had two sons—Abhishek and Raghav—both living abroad, working for IT companies. Kumar had a daughter whose name was Aaradhya, the only descendent of Ramani Uncle who was interested in the family's restaurant business. While he had never met Aaradhya, Kartik had seen her a number of times when she walked down the corner of Mysuru Ahara after parking her car inside the lane, on her way to Madras Meals. The girl was truly beautiful. How could she not be? After all, she resembled her paternal aunt, Janani.

He sighed when he recalled Janani's face; a face that continued to haunt him while awake and in his dreams. How could he forget her? Or the night they had spent together at his friend's empty house? It was a quirk of fate that the flat had been empty when Janani demanded that he make love to her. And he had access to the key. It was her one wish which he couldn't deny. And after that, they had never contacted one another.

He had her cell number saved on his smart phone. He hadn't been able to resist doing that when he got the opportunity at one of her art exhibitions. Of course, he had gone there when he had been sure that she wouldn't be around; just as he did every time there was an exhibition of her art works in town. In fact, he had a small collection of her paintings in his bedroom. How could he not? It was his only connection with the woman he loved from the bottom of his heart.

Kartik took an unscheduled off that afternoon, much to the manager Dayaram's surprise. After all, Kartik Hegde lived and breathed Mysuru Ahara and never, ever took a break from it. Getting into his car, he drove over to Inorbit Mall.

He reached The Oriental Bowl and lifted a hand to wave at Advik, who walked over to him immediately. "You are early, *Chitthaiya,*" said Advik, surprised.

"I know. I can wait till you finish your work."

"Would you like to sit in my office?" asked Advik.

Kartik shrugged. "I'm okay here. If I am not in the way, that is."

Advik grinned, shaking his head. "Not at all." The restaurant had closed after lunch and the waiters were cleaning up the area and setting up the tables for the dinner crowd.

"Will you have coffee? Or something stronger?"

"Isn't it too early for that?" asked Kartik, lifting an eyebrow.

Advik grinned. "You look like you could do with a brandy."

Kartik gave a nod, his face serious. "You are right about that."

"Let me get you a hot toddy," offered Advik before walking across to the bar. He went behind to quickly mix the drink, just the way he knew his uncle liked it. "Here you go," he said, placing the cocktail flavoured with nutmeg and cinnamon and sweetened with honey on the table.

Kartik took a sip before leaning back in his chair and crossing his legs, visibly relaxing. "Aah! This is perfect," he said, raising the glass to his nephew in a toast before taking another sip.

"So! What do you know about the Iyers?" asked Advik, coming to the point immediately. After all, he was at his work place and might be called to his station any moment. It was too early to take a coffee break right now.

"Who is this girlfriend you mentioned?"

"Aaradhya Iyer," said Advik briefly.

"You love her?" asked Kartik, taking a huge swallow of his drink.

Advik shrugged. "I'm not sure. Why do you ask?"

"How come she's your girlfriend if you don't love her?" asked Kartik, a scowl on his face as he glared at his nephew.

Advik shrugged again. "She's a girl and also happens to be my friend. But that's not the point, *Chitthaiya*. What do you know about the Iyers?"

Kartik sighed, shaking his head. The present generation was truly very different from his own. He wondered how close Advik was to this Aaradhya, but didn't ask him anything further on the subject. He didn't think his nephew would appreciate either his curiosity or his questions. "You must have heard of the legendary story of your grandfather and Ramani Iyer being partners many years ago?"

"I vaguely remember hearing about it from Akshatha *Ajji*. There was some kind of fallout in the partnership, right?"

"It was nothing as simple as that, believe me," said Kartik bitterly. "Can I have another one of this?"

"Did you drive over here, *Chitthaiya*?" asked Advik, lifting a hand to the bartender who had just walked into the restaurant.

"Yes. So?" he asked belligerently.

Advik refrained from replying, handing over the glass to the bartender and requesting him to get another toddy for the guest. Turning back to his uncle, he said mildly, "You shouldn't have another drink if you are driving."

"Says who? I have driven after even four pegs during those days, you know?"

Advik grinned. "Those were different days, *Chitthaiya*. It's illegal now. If you are caught…"

"Maybe they will put me in jail. What does it matter? I'll only be exchanging one for another, right?" He shrugged.

Advik sighed, changing the subject. "About the Iyers…?"

"Oh yes! It was not a simple fallout. I was in love with Ramani Uncle's daughter, Janani Iyer. To tell you the truth, I am still in love with her. We wanted to get married and her father was all for the idea. Ramani Uncle and Savitri Aunty came home to ask for my hand for their daughter. *Amma,* your dear grandmother, insulted both of them so terribly. It wasn't as if Savitri Aunty was quiet. They traded some fiery insults while the rest of us watched on. Both your grandfather and Ramani Uncle were too shocked to open their mouths, I think. Whatever, by the end of the horrific argument, there was no choice but for the Hegdes and Iyers to go our separate ways." He shuddered when he recalled the scene that was so deeply embedded in his consciousness and still managed to shake him up. After all, it was that moment when it had hit him hard that Janani was never going to be his.

Advik stared at his uncle in shock. "*Ajji* and the other lady quarrelled. *Ajja* and that uncle broke their partnership. All that I can understand. But why didn't you marry the woman you loved?"

"But how?" asked Kartik, glaring at his nephew as if it was all his fault. He had finished his second drink by now and lifted a hand for a third one. "The quarrel began with that only, *na*? *Amma* felt that the Iyer family wasn't good enough for the Hegdes. She was the one who insisted that a match wasn't possible between the two of us. As for *Appa,* he didn't like the idea because we belonged to different communities. He..."

"What?" Advik stared at his uncle in confusion. "I don't get it. What's the big deal with this community thingy? You are both Hindus, right?"

Kartik shook his head. "Those days, Advik…"

"It's still ridiculous, *Chitthaiya*. This was in the mid 90s, right? Not as if a century has gone by." Advik couldn't stop himself from becoming angry on his uncle's behalf.

Kartik sighed. "It was all my rotten luck that I never got a chance to marry Janani."

"Is it too late now?" asked Advik.

"Huh? What?" asked Kartik, confused.

"Is it too late to marry this lady you love? What I mean is, is she married to someone else?"

Kartik shook his head vigorously, a soft smile spreading across his face. "No, she's single, same as I am."

Advik jumped to his feet. "Then what's the problem, *Chitthaiya*? Why don't you marry her now?"

"Don't be an idiot, Advik. I don't think it's possible. I…"

"When are you going to realise that your life is in your hands, *Chitthaiya*? And not in your father's?"

Kartik met his nephew's steady gaze before lowering his own with a sigh. "You don't understand, Advik. But then, you are too smart to fall into your grandfather's trap. You insisted on being paid a salary. As for your father, Ganesh listens to everything the great Bhaskar Hegde says and hence has no problem. It is I, who's caught in the middle. I don't know how to rebel like you do; nor do I know how to completely toe the line like your father. You know how it is, no? I am caught between the rock and a hard place."

"*Chitthaiya*, listen." Advik placed a hand on his uncle's arm. "The past is gone and we cannot go back and change it. But the present and future are right here in front of you. I think you should seriously consider getting married. I can help you, if you will let me. I…"

Kartik looked up at his nephew, hope peeping out of his gaze for a couple of seconds before the light dimmed. Shaking his head, he said, "It's too late, my boy; too late."

Finally, Advik had to sign off early to drive his uncle back to his home, all because Kartik was too drunk to even take a few steps without falling on his face.

Advik held his uncle by the waist to make sure that he didn't fall down when he rang the bell to his grandfather's home in Bandra. He had already phoned his father and informed him about the circumstance. The door opened almost immediately, Ganesh standing on the other side, a frown on his face.

"What happened?" he asked, looking from his son to his brother and then back to his son.

"*Chitthaiya* had a couple of drinks, Dad. I think he's also extremely tired and that's why…"

"You mean two drinks too many; more than his usual three pegs?" Ganesh's frown deepened as he shook Kartik by his shoulder.

Advik gave a nod, not admitting that it had been way more than that. But then, Kartik had been terribly upset, recollecting his bitter past. He couldn't really blame his uncle. "Can you manage to take him inside?" he asked instead.

Ganesh turned inside to call a manservant who lived in. Damu came rushing to his employer's bidding. Grasping the situation immediately, he threw an arm around Kartik's waist and led him away.

"The car keys, Dad." Advik stood outside the threshold, offering Kartik's car keys to his father.

"Aren't you coming in?" asked Ganesh.

Advik smiled. "You know I can't."

"Damn it! It's my house too," growled Ganesh.

"Dad, please!" Advik placed a pacifying hand on his father's shoulder. "I... forget it, Dad. Why don't you and Mom meet me for lunch tomorrow?"

Ganesh gave a deep sigh before nodding. "Okay. Send me the name of the restaurant. I'll come along with Vrunda."

Advik gave his father a wide smile. Taking his hand, he pulled Ganesh out of the apartment to give him a hug. "I love you, Dad."

"I love you too, my son." Ganesh hugged his son tightly for a few minutes before reluctantly letting him go.

"Good night, Dad."

It took Advik only a few minutes to reach his building and he wasn't really surprised to find Aaradhya waiting for him inside his apartment. After all, he had given her a spare key.

"Hey!"

"Hey, yourself!" She flew into his arms before lifting her face for his kiss. Aaradhya was surprised when her ardent lover of the past few nights moved away after giving her the briefest of kisses. "Is everything okay?" she asked, giving him a sharp glance.

Advik took her hand and pulled her down to the sofa before sitting close to her. "Do you know that both our grandfathers used to be partners in the restaurant business?" he asked her.

Leaning her head on his shoulder, she gave a small nod. "I had heard about it vaguely before. Now I know the torrid details from my aunt, Janaki." She turned her face to look at his tense profile. "Do you know that my aunt is still in love with Kartik Hegde? That's probably…"

"…my uncle. Kartik *Chitthaiya* is my father's younger brother. He came over to my restaurant today. He was two hours early for our coffee date. The man is broken, Aara." A shuddering sigh broke out of the depths of Advik's being before he continued, "So much so that he got drunk. I know my uncle is fond of drinking, but I've never seen him like this. Fuck!" He jumped up from the sofa to walk to the end of the living room and back again. "He loves your aunt too."

Janaki shook her head. "This is such a waste, both of them holding a candle to each other, but unable to be together. Listen, can't we do something?" she asked, getting up to stand in front of him.

"Like what? I asked my uncle outright. Told him that he should get married to the woman he loved; at least now. But…"

"What did he say?" asked Aaradhya eagerly.

"That it's too late. Tch!" There was a bitter droop to Advik's lips. "I feel like picking up a fight with my grandfather. But the old man refuses to see me. He doesn't even let me inside the family home."

"What?" Aaradhya was shocked when she heard Advik's words. "Are you serious?" She had taken her grandparents' love—especially her grandfather's—for granted all through her life. How could Advik's grandfather do this to him?

"Of course I am. Otherwise I wouldn't be saying something as ridiculous as that, would I?" His jaw clenching in temper, he quickly told her the story of his refusing to follow his grandfather's diktat. "I wanted to learn all about world cuisine, but my *Ajja* felt that there was nothing to learn as he had already taught me all there is to know about Kannada cuisine. Isn't it a joke? *Ajja* believes that it is the sum total of what one needs to know about food."

Aaradhya stepped closer to throw her arms around Advik's waist, hugging him close. She could completely understand where he was coming from. It looked like Bhaskar Hegde had to answer for a lot of pain and bitterness in his descendants, all because of his stubborn nature. "Couldn't your grandmother talk your grandfather out of his conviction?" she asked.

Advik didn't reply to that. After all, Akshatha's silence had hurt him way more than Bhaskar's shouting. The grandmother who had loved him until the day he had announced he was going to the US to study further, had suddenly taken an about turn, taking his grandfather's side. What Advik wasn't aware of was that Akshatha hated his mother Vrunda, and the influence she had over her son. A typical mother-in-law, she didn't want her daughter-in-law to be given any kind of importance. While she had tolerated her son, Ganesh, loving his wife and listening to her counsel many a time, she couldn't digest it when Advik turned to his mother for all kinds of things.

All these days, Advik had managed to keep his chin up, extremely busy with his work. And there was also the time he spent with Aaradhya. That had really kept him happy. But today, meeting his father across the threshold, unable to step into the family home, had truly dragged down Advik's mood to the lowest level.

"Did you have dinner?" asked Aaradhya suddenly.

He shook his head. "Didn't feel like."

"Come and sit down." Aaradhya pushed him down on the sofa. "I haven't had dinner either. Let me rustle something up in your kitchen. Something light, okay?"

"Aara…"

"Shh." She placed a hand over his mouth, giving him a soft smile. "I'm not going to listen." She walked away before he could say anything more.

It was barely twenty minutes later when Aaradhya stepped to the living room entrance to call Advik, who had been staring at the ceiling. "Come on. Dinner's ready."

He got up reluctantly to drag his feet to the kitchen. But his stomach gave a hungry growl when he caught the aroma of *egg burji* and piping hot *rotis*. "That was fast," he said.

She grinned at him. "It's a simple meal. I'm sure you could have made it faster."

A glimmer of a smile broke out on Advik's face as he gave her a hug. "Thanks, babe."

She gave him a wink and sat next to him, sipping a glass of fresh lime juice that she had also made.

"Aren't you eating?" he asked, guzzling down the food on his plate, realising how hungry he was.

She patted her flat stomach, shaking her head. "Not after the *masala dosa* I ate at home."

"Liar!"

"Huh! It's the truth."

He shook his head. "I meant before. You lied to me that you were hungry and needed dinner."

She grinned shamelessly. "How else to make you agree to eat?'

He took her hand in his before lifting it to his lips and pressing a gentle kiss in the centre of her palm. "I think I'm falling in love with you," he admitted, his voice a hoarse whisper.

She jumped to her feet, pumping her fist in the air. "Finally! Finally, he admits he's in love with me," she hollered, dancing around the kitchen, her excitement obvious.

Advik laughed, sitting back in his chair, having polished off the food on his plate. How she made him happy, his Aaradhya!

14

Bhaskar was standing at the doorway to his bedroom when Ganesh climbed up the stairs to the second level of their duplex flat. "What happened?" asked Bhaskar, a deep scowl pleating his forehead as he minutely studied his elder son's face.

"Why? Nothing." Ganesh shrugged, refusing to meet his father's gaze. His temper was too high just then and he didn't want to lose it. After all, he had spent his whole life under his father's thumb and things weren't going to change overnight. Why kick up a storm now, after more than half a century?

"Ganesh!" Bhaskar's voice was soft, but like a whiplash nonetheless.

Ganesh stopped in his tracks, right in front of his father, his head bowed.

"Who was at the door?"

"Kartik," he muttered in response to his father's question.

"What happened to his key?" asked Bhaskar shrewdly.

Ganesh shrugged. "I don't really know. You will have to ask him tomorrow morning."

"Why not now?"

"He's too drunk to be able to understand anything."

"How did he reach home?" asked the father.

"I didn't ask, *Appa*. As I said before, he was in no state to answer questions."

"He came alone?"

Ganesh shrugged again, not uttering a word. After all, there was a difference in lying by omission and lying by commission.

"Answer me, Ganesh. I heard voices." Bhaskar did not want to take his grandson's name, though he was sure he had heard his grandson's voice. He had even felt his heart melting to an extent. But then, not enough to invite the boy inside his home.

"That was Damu. I had to call him to take Kartik to his room."

"Are you sure Kartik came home alone?"

"I suppose he did. At least, there was no one with him." There, he had just done it; lied to his father, by commission. And no, neither the thunder had struck nor lightning had bolted down the house. Ganesh took a deep breath, feeling a sense of freedom stealing over him.

Bhaskar realised that he wasn't going to get another word out of his elder son. Unable to mention Advik's name, all because of his mammoth ego and the restraints he had placed over himself, Bhaskar let go of the matter. "Okay."

"Goodnight, *Appa*." Ganesh walked on, further down the corridor to his room, his shoulders slouched in defeat. He realised that he didn't want to live separately from his son. Come morning, he intended telling his father exactly that.

But the morning had other plans it seemed.

Bhaskar spent an uneasy night in his bed, twisting and turning as he kept waking up again and again.

"Are you alright, Bhaskar?" asked Akshatha, getting up to sit on the bed next to her husband. She was too damn irritated with her husband for spoiling her sleep, all because of his restlessness.

"Not really," responded Bhaskar, his voice hoarse. He was sweating crazily despite the air-conditioner running full blast. "I'm feeling hot."

"Hot?" she yelled. "It's so damn cold in this bedroom that it can pass off for Antarctica."

"Give me the damn remote and get out of here," he ordered.

Akshatha was tempted to blast her husband then and there. But she stopped herself when she noticed his forehead beaded with sweat. It looked like Bhaskar was really feeling hot. She took the AC remote from her bedside table and reduced the temperature to eighteen degrees before handing it over to him. "Here, keep this next to you in case you want to change the temperature. I'm going to sleep in the dressing room." She didn't wait for his reply before walking across the bedroom to let herself into the adjoining room. Was she glad that they had a bed installed in here!

Bhaskar continued to toss and turn for the next couple of hours before an uneasy sleep claimed him just before dawn.

Akshatha walked into the bedroom at eight, surprised that her husband was still in bed at such a late hour. After all, Bhaskar tended to wake up by around five every morning.

"Bhaskar!" She walked towards the bed, calling his name. When he didn't open his eyes, she shook his shoulder and was startled when his right arm fell down the side of the bed. "Bhaskar?" She lifted his arm and placed it at his side on the bed. Or at least tried to. Only it fell back once again, hanging at the side. "Bhaskarrrrrrrrr!"

Ganesh came rushing into his parents' bedroom when he heard his mother's scream, followed by Vrunda. Kartik slowly walked in their wake, holding his head as he was suffering from a granddaddy of a headache.

"Ganesh, Kartik," Akshatha screamed, tears pouring down her face as she beat her chest. "Your father is dead," she declared.

Ganesh rushed forward to take his father's hand to check his pulse. While his father's arm weighed heavily in his hand, he could still feel a pulse, albeit weak. "*Amma*, stop crying. *Appa* is alive." He pulled out the mobile from his pocket and called for an ambulance. The next call was to the family doctor who didn't live far. Dr Paritosh Biswas came within five minutes. He had been sitting down to breakfast when the call came and came literally running down the street as he lived only a couple of buildings away.

"Bhaskar uncle has suffered a stroke," he said after checking the Hegde patriarch. "I've given him an injection for now. Which hospital do you plan to admit him to?"

"I was going to ask you that, Paritosh." Ganesh's hands were clutched into fists as he gave his school friend an anxious glance.

Paritosh patted him on his shoulder. "Take him to Lilavati. I'll call them immediately and book a room."

"The ambulance is here." Damu stepped into the room to inform Ganesh.

Ganesh accompanied his father in the ambulance, requesting Paritosh to follow as soon as he could. He also called his son, Advik, to inform him about the situation.

"I'll meet you at Lilavati, Dad," said Advik immediately on hearing about his grandfather's paralytic attack.

Ganesh hadn't expected anything less of his son. With a relieved smile on his face, he said, "I'll see you then, son."

It was four days before Bhaskar opened his eyes. The first thing he saw was his grandson sitting by his bedside. Tears ran down the corners of his eyes to drip into his pillow as he stared pathetically at the young man he had once upon a time, loved from the bottom of his heart. That was until the day when Advik went against his wishes to study in America. Looking back, Bhaskar felt rather stupid. Why had he stopped the younger man from flying free, soaring high? It had only been his ego, and nothing else. It was so sad that it was he, Bhaskar, who had created the rift between the two of them and allowed it to get wider and wider.

I shouldn't have ordered Advik to stay out of my home! After all, it is Advik's home too! Wisdom came not with age, but with a visit to death's door. Yes! That's what had happened to Bhaskar. He had almost died that night. He had been sure that he had stopped breathing for a couple of minutes; maybe longer, he wasn't sure. But he had felt an excruciating pain on one side of his body before his right arm and right leg had gone completely numb. He had tried to call out, but no sound had come out of his mouth, except for a guttural noise along with a lot of spittle. His lips had gone slack as he completely lost control over his facial muscles. Except for his eyes which could move. He had rolled his eyes, but what was the use? Even his wife wasn't around to see him, as it had been he who had told her to get out of the room in the middle of the night.

Bhaskar wasn't sure if he had slid into sleep or had fainted after some time, only to wake up in the hospital just now.

Advik had already moved back into the family home when Bhaskar was discharged a few days later. He spent most of his free time with his grandfather, while also continuing with his job.

"Why do you need the job now, Advik?" asked Ganesh, glad to have his son home, even if his father had to fall ill before that could happen.

Advik laughed, turning to meet his uncle's gaze before looking at his father. "Come on, Dad. I didn't take the job because *Ajja* wouldn't let me near Mysuru Ahara and you know that. You don't think I'm going to give up my dream just because *Ajja* fell ill, do you?"

There was a determined thrust to Advik's square chin as he looked his father in the eye.

Vrunda laughed softly, feeling so proud of her son. Ganesh turned to glare at his wife before looking at his son. "You still plan to…"

"…to branch out on my own in global cuisine, yes," said Advik firmly.

Ganesh glared at Kartik when he clapped loudly. "Why? I'm proud of my nephew. He truly knows what he's doing. And you know something, Ganesh, he's not like you and me. He's his own master."

"Meaning you and I aren't masters of our own lives?"

"Hehe! Exactly."

Ganesh sighed, unable to deny his brother's words. But he so didn't want his father and his son to clash with each other. He was getting too old and tired for this.

"Dad!" Advik went forward to throw his arm around his father's shoulders. "You shouldn't worry, Dad. I can convince *Ajja*. And I promise not to quarrel with him, okay?"

Ganesh lifted his worried gaze to his son's soothing one. "Are you sure?"

"Believe me, yes."

Bhaskar's recovery was slow, but steady. He had a full-time nurse and a visiting physiotherapist who helped him with his exercises. At eighty-two, any other person would have thrown in the towel and waited to breathe his last. But not Bhaskar! He was determined to recover completely. After all, he had to ask for his grandson's forgiveness, in so many words!

15

"*Thatha*, are you busy?" Aaradhya stepped inside Ramani's study the early next morning to see him working on an account book. It was one of the two days in a week when he worked from home in the mornings. Ramani didn't really understand the meaning of the term 'holiday'. He loved his work so much that he kept at it day after day after day.

Ramani looked up and smiled. "No, my child. Come along and sit down." He patted the chair at his side, closing the notebook to give her his complete attention.

"Um… er… *Thatha*… I…"

"Are you in love?" asked Ramani, a twinkle in his gaze.

Aaradhya burst out laughing, jumping to her feet to give him a hug. "You are too much, *Thatha*. How did you guess so easily?"

"So? I was right. That's not so difficult, little one. You have not hesitated to tell me anything, never before now."

"And that's how you caught me out. Do you want to know about Advik?" she asked, sitting back down on the chair.

"Everything, yes." A shadow passed over his face when he recalled a similar conversation with his daughter Janani all those years ago. Mentally shaking his head, he pulled himself out of morbid thoughts. Never! *Aaradhya will get married and lead a wonderful life with the man she loved,* he swore to himself.

Taking a deep breath, Aaradhay plunged in, speaking fast, not giving her grandfather a chance to interrupt. "His name is Advik Hegde. He's also from a restauranteur family, same as we are. In fact, you used to know his grandfather Bhaskar Hegde really well. Advik..."

Ramani Iyer had tuned out off the rest of her conversation, the blood draining out of his face, leaving it completely pale. How could God be so cruel?! When Aaradhya's voice dwindled into silence, he gave her a pathetic glance. "My dear child! I don't know what to say. I..." He paused to take a deep breath before continuing, "Do you even have an idea of our history? The story between the Hegdes and our family? About Janaki..."

"*Thatha!*" Aaradhya placed a hand on her grandfather's arm. "I know everything, at least the main details. What I want to tell you is this: Advik and I haven't really thought that far. He's working on setting up a restaurant serving global cuisine and is doing his best towards achieving that goal. It's just that he's the man I love and he loves me too. And I want you to meet him. What we have decided is to get Janani *Athai* and his Kartik *Chitthaiya* married first. What do you say?"

A lone tear ran down Ramani's wrinkled cheek. "You don't know how huge a task you both have set yourself, my dear. Those days, Bhaskar and I were really close, closer than some brothers even. I still can't comprehend how it happened; how the partnership broke up so fast. Poor Janu," he sighed, "poor Janu was heartbroken. As a father, I've failed her."

"Please don't say that, *Thatha*. It wasn't your fault. And blaming anyone is not the solution anyway. Listen, there is more."

"What?"

She quickly told him all about Bhaskar having thrown his grandson out of the family home and the reason for it.

Ramani's heart went out to the young Advik. "When are you bringing your Advik to meet your family?" he asked.

Gentle colour flared up Aaradhya's cheeks when she heard her grandfather calling him 'her Advik'. "I want you to meet him first, *Thatha*. The others can meet Advik afterwards."

Ramani nodded his salt and pepper head, smiling at her. "Right. So, when?"

"Day after tomorrow? He has an off then."

"I'll be waiting," said Ramani, getting up from his chair. Placing a hand on his granddaughter's head he said, "God bless you, my child. I wish you all the happiness in the world."

Aaradhya hugged her grandfather as they stepped out of the study. "Don't mention anything to *Paati*, okay? I don't want her to worry unnecessarily."

He nodded, giving her a conspiratorial smile. "My lips are zipped," he said, drawing his thumb and forefinger across his mouth in a zipping gesture, making her laugh.

What Aaradhya did not foresee was for Advik to completely disappear off her radar.

Aaradhya thumbs moved quickly on the keyboard of her phone as she typed out a message to Advik on the Tinder chat box. "

Hey, just spoke to my grandfather. He's keen to meet you. Please come home for lunch the day after tomorrow. I can't tell you how excited I am.

Advik had not even seen the message, let alone replied to it—not even after four days. She even tried calling him; but he did not pick her calls.

What could have gone wrong? The last time they met, Advik had told her in so many words that he was falling in love with her. Had something happened to him? She began to get worried.

Aaradhya went to Oberoi Mall late the next night to catch him when he finished work. It was gone eleven thirty when he did not step out of the restaurant. She walked in, glad to see a few workers still around; though there were no customers at that late hour. Walking up to the cash counter, she asked, "Has Advik left?"

A man lifted his head from his laptop to look at her with a startled expression. "Advik Hegde?" When Aaradhya nodded, he said, "But ma'am, Advik went on leave from yesterday."

She blanched on hearing that, convinced by now that he was either ill or had had an accident. "Why?" she asked in a hoarse whisper, before explaining herself. "Did he say why he needed leave?"

"Some kind of a family emergency, ma'am. Do you want me to…?"

She shook her head vigorously, not keen to bother him anymore. "No, no, that's fine. And thanks."

"Any message I can give Advik?" asked the man, feeling sorry for the young woman. She looked really disturbed.

"No, nothing. I'll go," she muttered before rushing out of the restaurant.

What could have happened? And how to find out?

"I hope you remembered to invite your Advik for lunch at Madras Meals." Ramani Iyer spoke in a secretive whisper when they met at the breakfast table the next morning. He had been waiting for his wife Savitri to go to the kitchen as she was wont to do every half an hour or so.

Aaradhya lifted her pinched face to glance at her grandfather, her shoulders slouched in defeat. Shrugging, she said, "He's not free, *Thatha*." She didn't plan to admit to her grandfather that the man who was supposedly falling in love with her, was ignoring her royally. She didn't want to add to Ramani's anxiety as he kept comparing the situation to his daughter Janani's marriage that never materialised.

Ramani patted her hand that lay on the table. "So! Let's do it another day, my dear. There's no need to be heartbroken about it. You know how the restaurant business is, full of emergencies. He must have got caught up with something. Do cut him some slack, Aara."

"Sure, *Thatha,* I will. And I do understand. It's just that I'm so disappointed. I…"

Ramani shook his head, laughing. "Patience is definitely not your virtue, my child."

She wrinkled her nose at him, glad to drop the subject when her grandmother returned from the kitchen.

Aaradhya couldn't believe that it was more than forty-eight hours since she had spoken with Advik. He had not replied to her chat on the Tinder app; nor had he returned her calls. She had waited outside his workplace the earlier night, only to be told by the manager that he was on leave because of some family emergency.

She had rushed over to his apartment, only to find it locked. Where the hell was the man? He had not answered her calls, yes, four of them. Though she wasn't keen on making a nuisance of herself, she had given long gaps before each call. She paced the kitchen restlessly as she waited for the croissants to finish baking. What must have gone wrong?

Was it really a family emergency? Or had Advik decided that he didn't want her in his life any longer?

Somehow, Aaradhya couldn't believe the second reason. After all, their chemistry in bed was simply mind blowing. Why should he drop her suddenly like a hot potato? That must mean there was really a family emergency. And she was back to her earlier question: How to find out?

She paused in her track to snap her fingers. Kartik *Chitthaiya*! She knew he sat at the cash counter of Mysuru Ahara until six every day. She decided to pay him a visit. If Advik didn't care for the idea, too bad! She would rather he told her to her face if he wasn't interested in her any longer. But not ignoring her like this, as if she had ceased to exist. Her temper gave her the adrenalin boost to follow action to thoughts. She finished her baking and packed everything into appropriate cartons and send them off with the delivery man who had come over from Madras Meals. Changing out of her track pants and t-shirt, she pulled on a pair of jeans and cotton *kurti* before walking over to Mysuru Ahara which was barely ten minutes away from her home.

She smiled when she saw an older version of Advik at the counter. The man could either be his father or his uncle. Taking a chance, she stepped closer to speak to him. "Kartik *Chitthaiya*?" she enquired.

Kartik lifted his head from the cash register to see the woman he knew as Aaradhya standing in front of him, his eyes going wide. She was a younger version of Janani, and as beautiful as her aunt.

"That's right. And you must be Aaradhya," he said, a small smile spreading over his face.

"Yes." She looked at the man her aunt loved; finding it an effort to smile as she couldn't help thinking of Advik who was missing in action. "Er… I…"

"Is everything alright?" he asked, noticing the sadness lurking in her lovely eyes.

Aaradhya wrinkled her nose, giving a shake of her head, her smile disappearing altogether. "Not really, *Chitthaiya*. Will it be possible to speak to you in private?"

Kartik had a good mind to give his nephew a kick on his ass the next time he met him, which would be the same evening. By now, he was sure it was Advik's fault that this young lady was appearing so dejected. "Why don't you find an empty table? I'll join you in five minutes."

"I'll do that," said Aaradhya before turning around, her eyes searching for a table. It was next to impossible in the rush hour, but she pounced when she saw a couple getting up to leave. She quickly dived in to sit down on the vacant chair. She lifted a hand to Advik's uncle after settling down.

Kartik waved right back before stepping out from behind the counter after making sure Dayaram had taken charge. He slid into the chair opposite before asking, "What will you have?"

Her throat working with deep emotion, she said, "Nothing for me."

"Come on, young lady. You must have something. Coffee?" When she nodded, he hailed a waiter and ordered two coffees and a plate of *pakoras*. "They are the best *pakoras* this side of town," he said, grinning mischievously.

Aaradhya smiled through her anxiety, giving him a nod.

"So! Tell me. What did you want to speak to me about?"

"*Chitthaiya*! Is there some kind of a family emergency?" asked Aaradhya, coming directly to the point.

"Aah!" Kartik sat back in his chair. "That's right. How did you know?"

She looked at him anxiously. Ignoring his question, she asked, "What's wrong?"

Kartik sighed. "My father, Bhaskar Hegde, suffered a paralytic stroke. He's in hospital. The doctor says he is getting better. But he hasn't opened his eyes in the past forty-eight hours."

Her hands on her cheeks, Aaradhya lifted her horrified gaze to Kartik's. "Oh my God! Advik must be terribly upset."

Kartik couldn't help smiling on hearing her words. She was so engrossed with her boyfriend's reaction. "He's heartbroken," he said softly. "He's always adored his grandfather. And the separation hasn't done either of them any good."

Aaradhya nodded, well aware of how much Advik was hurt by his grandfather keeping him out of his family home.

"Maybe it's all for the best," continued Kartik, pushing the plate of *pakoras* towards her. "My father falling ill. Sometimes, these things bring people closer. Don't you agree?"

Aaradhya gave him a dazed look, realising that he was probably right. "Does that mean Advik is with his grandfather right now?"

Kartik smiled. "Yes. He wouldn't let anyone else stay with his favourite *Ajja* and has parked himself at the hospital twenty-four by seven."

"Oh!"

"Go on, taste the *pakoras*. Or you'll never know that it's way better than what is served at Madras Meals," he teased, giving her a wink.

Aaradhya laughed, feeling way lighter after knowing the reason for Advik distancing himself from her. He was busy with his grandfather and here she had been imagining that he had dumped her. Popping a *pakora* into her mouth, she closed her eyes to savour it. "Mmm… this is yum."

"Isn't it better?" asked Kartik.

"*Chitthaiya*! You are teasing me. But if you want to know the truth, it tastes exactly the same as what we serve at Madras Meals."

He sighed, shaking his head. "Exactly. Both the restaurants have the same roots, don't they?" He sighed again; this time louder. "It's so bloody sad, this rift."

She placed a hand over his, not knowing what to say. She was only too aware now of the lost love between her aunt and Advik's uncle. How she wished she could do something about it!

"It truly is, *Chitthaiya*. My grandfather still loves your father; still thinks of him as a close friend; closer than all his other associates in this city."

"Ramani Uncle always had a big heart." Kartik rubbed his hands over his eyes, refusing to let himself cry at all the pain both the families had undergone. What a waste!

"Kartik!"

He turned to see his elder brother standing next to him, though Ganesh's eyes were on the young woman sitting on the opposite side of the table.

"Ganesh! This is Aaradhya…"

"…Iyer. I suppose you are Janani's niece?" asked Ganesh, convinced he was right. The young lady was the spit image of her aunt.

"Yes, Uncle. I…"

"This is my elder brother, Ganesh," said Kartik, completing the introductions.

Advik's father! Aaradhya didn't know what to say, how to react. She turned to give Kartik a helpless glance.

"Aaradhya is Advik's friend." Kartik threw the cat among the pigeons. Well, his brother had to know, sometime.

"Is that so? Nice to meet you, young lady," said Ganesh, offering his hand for a shake. He decided then and there that if Advik was in love with this young woman, he, Ganesh, was not going to allow history to repeat itself. He had had up to there of the enmity between the Iyers and Hegdes. "You must be Kumar's daughter?"

"That's right, Uncle," said Aaradhya, giving him a shaky smile.

"How is your grandfather, Ramani Uncle?"

"He's fine, Uncle. And I am sorry to hear about Bhaskar *Ajja's* stroke. I hope he recovers soon."

Ganesh gave his brother a twinkling glance before turning to the woman in front of him. Bhaskar *Ajja* indeed! "Thank you, Aaradhya. You must convey my regards to your grandfather. I'll leave you both to finish your conversation. And do feel free to visit us more often."

"Thank you, Uncle," said Aaradhya, her smile wider now. "Advik's father is nice," she told Kartik once Ganesh walked away from their table.

"Better than his uncle?" asked Kartik, tongue firmly in cheek.

"*Chitthaiya!*" Aaradhya laughed. Sobering up, she said, "I want to meet Advik."

Kartik sighed. "I don't know, Aara. I don't think Advik is going to thank me for interfering. But just now, he's in a bad space and might not be open to meeting anyone other than family. Let my father wake up. I'll give you a call. And maybe I can take you when I go to the hospital. Give it a few days, hmm?"

Aaradhya didn't like what she heard, but she could see the sense in Kartik's words. "Okay, *Chitthaiya*. Thank you."

"For what, my dear?" he asked, getting up from his chair.

"For your patience, for listening to me. I think I've fallen in love with him," she confessed, her voice a whisper.

"Aah!" He gave her a hug. "My nephew is truly lucky. I only hope he realises it. Or I might take pleasure in bashing it into his head."

Aaradhya's mouth fell open before she realised that he was joking. Shaking her head at him, she took her leave, walking out of the restaurant, happier than when she had walked inside.

16

Four days earlier, Advik had received the shock of his life when his father called and told him that his grandfather, Bhaskar Hegde, had suffered a paralytic stroke. He couldn't believe his ears. He hadn't met his grandfather in almost six years. But he knew how healthy the old man was. His eating habits were well disciplined and he always made it a point to take a brisk walk for at least half an hour every day. He was also careful not to consume too much non-vegetarian food items; preferring chicken and fish over red meat. He also had regular health check-ups and the only tablets he consumed were multi-vitamins.

How had he suddenly had a paralytic attack? Advik had thrown on some clothes and rushed to the hospital soon after his father's call. He had called his boss to take a few days off before waiting for his grandfather to be brought to his room after the battery of tests that he seemed to require.

Advik had sent his father and uncle home, insisting on remaining at his grandfather's bedside, his hands held together in silent prayer. No! He would not cry. Crying meant that he was admitting defeat. He would not let his grandfather's health deteriorate further. But sitting at Bhaskar's bedside, day and night, waiting for him to open his eyes, had shaken Advik up a lot.

He held his grandfather's frail hand between his own strong ones, trying to breathe life into the still old man, checking the monitors from time to time as if to make sure that they were still running. What if he stopped breathing before Advik could apologise?

Please God! Give me just the one chance to say I am sorry! And how much I love him! Advik pleaded with the Almighty.

The second day, coming to a sudden conclusion, Advik began to speak to his grandfather, who was still in a comatose state. But he didn't care. Maybe his grandfather's soul might hear him. So he spoke to the comatose Bhaskar, a lot.

"I am sorry, *Ajja*. I'm really sorry that I went off to the US without giving you fair warning. I should have given you time to prepare. After all, I had been planning the trip for almost a year. But *Ajja,* I was scared. I was scared that you might stop me from doing what I wanted. That still is no excuse for keeping you in the dark. I love you *Ajja,* from the bottom of my heart. And I respect you deeply. This passion I have for cooking, I have got it from you *Ajja*. Do you remember the time when you began taking me to Mysuru Ahara's kitchen? I was barely seven. But you let me help you knead the dough and peel carrots and cucumbers. I loved it all, *Ajja*. I…" Advik choked, his throat clogging with emotion. He took a few sips of water before continuing to speak to his sleeping grandparent. He wasn't going to let him die.

His grandmother Akshatha visited each evening and stayed for about a couple of hours. "So, you remembered your old grandparents?" she asked on the first day.

Advik turned blazing eyes to his grandmother. "No *Ajji*. I didn't remember," he responded firmly.

"Huh! What do you mean?" She glared at him. She had enjoyed spoiling the young Advik and had showered him with a lot of gifts. But Akshatha didn't really know how to show affection to people, anyone in the family.

"I had to forget you both in the first place, didn't I?" he asked in a gentle voice. He knew her for what she was and still loved her. She was, after all, his father's mother. "It wasn't my decision to stay away, *Ajji*. And you very well know it."

She sighed loudly. "It's all because of the evil eye. Everyone is jealous of our family."

Advik couldn't help smiling on hearing her words. Akshatha strongly believed in the evil eye and that was the reason she came up with, whenever there was an insurmountable problem.

"What are you grinning about?" she accused.

"Nothing, *Ajji*." He went forward to give her a hug. She was a cantankerous old woman, but she was still his grandmother.

Kartik walked in just then, having arrived directly from the restaurant. He handed a parcel of hot *upma* and *pineapple sheera* to his nephew along with a flask of filter coffee.

"What did you bring?" asked Akshatha eagerly. She loved food and it didn't really matter if she was hungry or not. Kartik, who was only too aware of his mother's eating habits, had brought enough to feed an army.

"I'm sure you won't like it, *Amma*," he teased, turning to give his nephew a wink.

"How will you know?" Akshatha glared at her younger son before turning eagerly to her grandson. "Advik?"

Advik served the food on two plates and handed one to his grandmother. "What about you, *Chitthaiya*?" he asked, tucking into his own plate.

"I'm full," said Kartik, patting his flat stomach. "How is *Appa*?" he asked, turning to gaze at his father's supine form.

"Same as yesterday," said Advik, pouring himself a cup of coffee. "Will you have some, *Ajji*?" he turned to ask his grandmother.

She shook her head. "Not for me. I can't sleep if I have coffee so late in the day."

"Would you like something cold? I can bring something from the canteen."

Her eyes lit up. "I would like to have *Maaza*."

Kartik rolled his eyes before getting up.

"You sit down, *Chitthaiya*. I'll go get it. I need to stretch my legs anyway," Advik offered.

Kartik looked at his nephew's cheerless face and sighed. The old man was killing his grandson with guilt. That much was obvious to him. But there was nothing he could do about it. "Alright. There's no need to rush back if you want to go for a walk. I'll keep *Amma* company."

Akshatha looked from one to the other. Didn't either man realise that she was dying for a cold drink? But she didn't open her mouth when Advik left the hospital room.

Advik walked briskly for about twenty minutes before returning to the hospital, his mind occupied with thoughts of his sick grandfather. If he had checked his Tinder app, he might have seen multiple messages from Aaradhya. But he had switched off notifications for the app and didn't bother to open it. After all, now was not the time. He was like a hen sitting on eggs as his only focus was to get his grandfather up on his feet. Not that he could do anything about it as of now, but simply watch the old man as he lay there on the hospital bed, all the different monitors ticking around him, reassuring Advik that his grandfather was still alive.

Buying a half litre bottle of *Maaza* at the hospital canteen, he went back to his grandfather's hospital room. Opening the bottle cap, he handed the cold drink to his grandmother.

"How's Aaradhya?" asked Kartik in a soft voice, not to let his mother hear him.

Advik turned to scowl at his uncle before shrugging. "I don't really know. Why do you ask?"

"What? Isn't she your girlfriend?" asked Kartik, his forehead pleating in a frown.

Advik shrugged again. "I suppose you can call her that. But we aren't committed to one another." He hadn't bothered to speak to Aaradhya, not since his grandfather's hospitalisation the earlier morning. Nor was she aware that he was on leave. But then, he wasn't really answerable to her, was he? He had made it clear that he had no place in his life for a long-term relationship. They had liked each other; they had had a good time. But not any longer.

No, he was not going to think about the last words he had spoken to her. *I think I'm falling in love with you*. How he wished he could retract those words. Wrong timing, that's what it was. If he had waited a few more hours, he wouldn't have uttered them, and consequently, she wouldn't have any expectations from him.

Even now, what did it matter? He had only said he thought he was in love with her. He had not declared his love for her. And what the hell was this love everyone harped so much about? It could only lead to unhappiness. Look at his Kartik Uncle for example. What had he achieved by holding a candle to Janani Iyer? Not a damn thing but heartache.

Advik had more than enough on his plate what with his grandfather fighting for his life in the hospital. Agreed that he was eighty-two years old and had lived his life well. But Advik missed the old man, terribly. They had not spoken as much as a word between them in the past six years. He felt like crying whenever he thought about it, the guilt smothering him. This was no time to think of a woman who may or may not become a part of the rest of his life.

"Oh!" Kartik was startled to hear his nephew's words. Though he really didn't understand what Advik meant. But before he could ask more questions, the doctor walked in, much to Advik's relief. After that, it was time for the visitors to leave. "I'll call you," said Kartik as he escorted his mother on their way out.

"Do that," said Advik. He planned to message the family group about his grandfather's health status and keep his phone on silent mode. He didn't want to speak to anybody, and he was clear that included everyone he knew. Yes, even Aaradhya.

She was a young woman who was cherished by her family. She enjoyed life and lived it to the full. Surely, she wouldn't want to be caught up in the complexities of the Hegdes' way of life? Look at her aunt! The woman had fallen in love with Kartik Hegde and she must surely be repenting it till date. Advik didn't want Aaradhya to be tainted by the same brush.

Right now, the focus was his grandfather and Advik wasn't keen to upset the old man, not more than was required. After all, he wasn't going to change his career plans which in itself might create another war in the Hegde household. He didn't want to pile that up with a love match that was bound to rub his grandfather the wrong way. Better to let go of Aaradhya before they got too close. It was best to break off from the relationship before it became any deeper.

But what about himself? Had he not begun to fall for her charms? Advik refused to think of it. One of the reasons why he had switched off his Tinder notifications. Aaradhya had called, four times since yesterday morning. He had not taken her calls. Nor had he bothered to call her back. He couldn't see the sense in prolonging the agony. It was best to make it a clean break. After all, hadn't he told her right in the beginning that he wasn't into long term relationships? She had better accept that they were not going to be together, not any more.

Then why the hell did he feel as if his heart was breaking in two?

Advik refused to delve into himself to seek an answer. Right now, it was important that he kept his focus completely on his grandfather.

But then, Providence played her own part, just the way she had meant to, fitting the roles of people into the gigantic divine jigsaw she had created exclusively for humanity.

Aaradhya didn't seek Advik's permission before walking right back into his life, though only after his grandfather stepped back on the road to recovery.

17

Bhaskar Hegde opened his eyes on the fourth day to see his grandson sitting beside his bed, holding his left hand in both of his. He opened his mouth to call out, "Advik," but no sound came out. He tried once again only to realise that neither his lips nor his vocal cords seemed to be in his control. Sweat poured from his forehead even as he felt smothered by panic, his heartbeat soaring high. He inadvertently pulled at his left hand.

Advik looked up when he felt a tug on his hands. Lifting his gaze to his grandfather's face, he smiled when he saw the old man's eyes were open. "*Ajja!* You are awake." He got up from his chair to step closer to his grandfather, leaning down to look into Bhaskar's eyes. "Hello *Ajja*! Good afternoon!" Advik spoke as if nothing had happened between them. That the years between, when they had not spoken a word with each other, didn't exist. "I'm glad to see you awake." He reached forward to kiss his grandfather's shrunken cheek before ringing the bell for the nurse.

He continued to speak. "Today is Friday and you have been in the hospital from Tuesday morning. It's three o' clock in the afternoon. Paritosh Uncle is treating you and he's confident you are on the road to recovery." Advik lifted a hand to run it over his grandfather's head in a gesture of affection. "I've missed you, *Ajja*."

The tears flowed fast as Bhaskar reached out his left hand to take Advik's in his, raising it to his lips.

Understanding the gesture for what it was, Advik smiled. "It's okay, *Ajja*. We go back a long way. In fact, from the moment I was born. I love you so much. You'd better get well soon. You owe me a number of tennis matches. I hope you realise that I won't let you back out of the challenge."

Bhaskar gave his grandson a lopsided smile through his tears. He realised at that moment that he was on the road to recovery. How could he not? He needed to live if he wanted to spend time with his favourite grandson.

The nurse walked in and smiled when she noticed that the patient's eyes were open. "Good afternoon, sir. I'm glad to see that you are awake at last. Let me call the doctor."

Paritosh came almost immediately, smiling at his patient. "Bhaskar Uncle, I knew you would come out of this. After all, you are really fit for someone your age. So, how are you feeling?" He chatted as he checked all the vitals before turning to Advik. "A few more days, Advik. Then your grandpa can go home. I've prescribed a different set of medicines. There's nothing to worry now. He should be fine." He patted his friend's son on his shoulder. Turning to his patient, he said, "You are lucky to have Advik for your grandson. He hasn't moved from your side from the time you came to the hospital."

Bhaskar's hold on his grandson's hand tightened all the more, his eyes overflowing with love and gratitude as he gazed at Advik.

"No more tears, *Ajja,*" whispered Advik, wiping his grandfather's face with tissues from the bedside table. "We should be celebrating actually. Let me call *Appa* and tell him that you are awake."

Ganesh came within half an hour, keen to meet his father and see for himself that he had really opened his eyes, after lying unmoving on the hospital bed for four days and nights. Advik had to wait outside as it wasn't visiting hours yet. Ganesh spent a few minutes with his father, bringing him up to date on the business front. "You should not worry about anything, *Appa*. We are managing well. I want you to completely recover first. I also spoke to Paritosh. He's really happy with your progress."

Bhaskar gave his elder son a frustrated glance. Couldn't Ganesh see that he couldn't speak? It was so damn infuriating.

Ganesh smiled when he noticed the irritation in his father's eyes. Placing a hand on the older man's shrunken shoulder, he said, "I know, *Appa*. But it's only a temporary thing. Paritosh is confident that you will regain your speech with the right treatment and exercises. Do be patient." But he knew that patience was one quality which Bhaskar had never possessed.

Kartik came in the evening along with his mother. After having a one-sided chat with his father for a couple of minutes, he turned to his nephew. "Want to step out with me for a while? I'm sure *Amma* wants to spend some private time with *Appa*."

Advik turned to his grandfather who gave him a nod, before walking out with his uncle.

"Listen, about Aaradhya..."

Advik stopped in his tracks to glare at his uncle. "What about Aaradhya?" he snarled. He was angry with her or at least that's what he had convinced himself of being. After all, how else could he explain away the hollow feeling within him whenever he thought of her? He had never wanted a relationship with her in the first place. But she had agreed that they would meet whenever they were both free and it was going to be nothing long term.

Well, now he was busy with family issues. And he could not simply take leave of absence indefinitely. He had a full-time job and a sick grandfather to take care of. He also needed to set right his relationship with his grandfather, now that he was back to the world of the living. He did not have time for a girlfriend.

"*Arre, itna badakthe kyun ho*?" asked Kartik, glaring right back at his nephew. "She's been trying to reach you these past days. You haven't even bothered to respond to her messages. She..."

"What is it to you? Or did she complain to you about me?" asked Advik, his temper mounting.

"Don't you dare take that tone with me, young man! I know that you modern people don't want us oldies to interfere. But I can't sit back and watch this nonsense. I..."

"What nonsense?" They had reached the cafeteria which was rather crowded. Advik turned around to leave the place, dragging his uncle by the hand.

"The pain Aaradhya is undergoing, all because of the way you have been ignoring her. She..."

"Don't be duh, *Chitthaiya*. I've been sitting with *Ajja*, anxious whether he was going to survive the stroke or not. You know that he hadn't opened his eyes in all of four days. How can I think of my "girlfriend"?" He drew quotation marks in the air as he quickly walked down the lane, without even bothering to check if his uncle was following him.

"So, you agree she's your girlfriend?"

Advik sighed, stopping suddenly in his tracks to turn around and glower at his uncle. "Are you being funny?"

"I can't see anyone laughing here," muttered Kartik.

"*Chitthaiya*! I don't have the bandwidth to deal with a girlfriend right now. I am worried about *Ajja*. I..."

"The rest of your life cannot come to a standstill just because your *Ajja* has fallen sick, Advik. And he's already on the way to recovery. Aara is not an object which you can ignore when you please and get back to after a break. She's also suffering in her own way, you know. She didn't even know what had happened. Whether you were angry with her or just disgusted with her. She didn't know why you wanted to break with her, if you did. The poor girl..."

"STOP. RIGHT. THERE!" They had reached a restaurant by now and walked inside, both sitting down to glare at each other. "Aaradhya is not a poor girl as you call her. She's smart and intelligent. And strong as well."

"Oh! I'm glad to hear that," said Kartik, highly sarcastic. "But that still didn't stop her from worrying why you were not talking to her all of a sudden."

Advik looked down at the table, a feeling of guilt creeping in. His uncle wasn't exactly wrong. But then… "You don't understand, *Chitthaiya*. I cannot spare the time. Forget time, I don't have the energy for a girlfriend. Don't you get it?"

Kartik shook his head. "Aara doesn't come across as someone who is all that demanding. If you ask my opinion…"

"I am not," muttered Advik.

Ignoring his nephew, Kartik continued, his voice louder than before, "If you ask my opinion, you should get in touch with her. This pressure you are feeling, believe me, she will help ease it. She's a wonderful girl, Advik. And she will be a perfect support for you under the circumstances. What if you both were already married? Will you ignore your wife in such an emergency?"

"That's different, *Chitthaiya*. I…" Advik jumped up from his chair to glare down at his uncle. "What's wrong with you? Why are you suddenly talking about marriage of all things? And you, who are still a bachelor in your cranky old age?"

"Stop insulting me, brat. And sit down. You're creating a scene."

Advik sat down reluctantly, doing his best to ignore the other customers in the restaurant who were beginning to look their way.

It took Kartik the better part of an hour, but he managed to convince his nephew that he was being ridden with guilt—regarding not just his grandfather, but also about his relationship with Aaradhya. "You need to lighten up, brat. You are taking care of your grandfather, good. But why ignore Aaradhya? Tell her about it. If she's being a support, well and good. Fair enough if she's indifferent. If she cribs too much, chuck her out of your life then. But you can't behave as if she doesn't exist. She more than exists; she has been a huge part of your life in the past couple of weeks, hasn't she?"

"You are a fine one to talk, *Chitthaiya*," said Advik, his temper gone, but a mild irritation still dogging his mind. "You…"

"Now, you stop right there, my boy! I have done some things that I truly regret. But I cannot go back to my past and set them right now, can I? How much ever I wish I could do it. But can't I at least help you with my voice of experience?"

Advik turned silent when he noticed the sad expression in his uncle's gaze. Sighing, he gave a nod. "Okay, you are right. I'll get in touch with Aara today itself."

"Now?" The sadness disappeared to be replaced by a mischievous twinkle.

"Don't push me too far," grumbled Advik, finishing his coffee.

They left, uncle and nephew, to return to the hospital, more at peace with the world after their heartfelt dialogue.

As they got out of the lift, Advik pressed his uncle's shoulder. "You are the best uncle a man could ask for." His voice was gruff and he refused to meet Kartik's knowing gaze.

Kartik laughed softly. "I know, man, I know." He stopped in his tracks to stand in front of Advik, his face turning serious. "I only wish I had been a more understanding boyfriend and less of an obedient son." He couldn't hide the bitterness from his face and voice.

"*Chitthaiya!*" Advik hugged the older man, having no reply to offer him.

18

During his grandfather's treatment period at the hospital, the most beautiful time in Advik's life were the hours he spent with Aaradhya. She asked him no questions, she offered no advice. She was simply there for him. There were times when she met him at the hospital cafeteria when Advik had a few minutes of respite. Or she went to his place of work, just when he was finishing for the day. An encouraging word and a peck on his cheek, just enough to keep him going through his long days at work and even longer nights in his grandfather's hospital room. She brought him a croissant she had baked or a piece of cake, bringing a smile to his morose face.

It was only yesterday Aaradhya had met him at the hospital cafeteria. "There's someone I'd like you to meet," she said mysteriously when she met him at the lift.

"Who would that be?" asked Advik, taking her hand in one of his own to lock his fingers with hers.

"Come with me." They stepped into the café and walked to a table for four.

Advik's stared with wide eyes when his gaze fell on the woman who was an older version of Aaradhya. "Will that be Janani Aunty?"

"Yes," said Aaradhya, a smile in her voice. "Janani *Athai*..."

Janani lifted a hand to her niece, stopping her in mid-sentence, a wide smile on her face. "This is your Advik, who is also my Kartik's nephew."

Aaradhya left the two of them to walk to the counter to place an order for three cups of coffee, her heart bubbling with excitement as she watched them from afar.

Advik laughed, taking Janani's hand and shaking it. "It's lovely meeting you. Janani *Athai*, right? Kartik *Chitthaiya* has told me all about you."

Her smile cooling, Janani asked sharply. "Oh! Did he now? I'm glad to know he hasn't completely forgotten me." Her chin lifted defiantly as she eyed the younger man. "But forget all that and tell me about your grandfather. Aara tells me that Bhaskar Uncle is recovering well."

Advik gave Janani a gentle smile, sitting down next to her. "That's right. *Ajja* is on the road to recovery. But getting back to Kartik *Chitthaiya*, he still loves you, *Athai*. In fact, I've been chasing him..." he paused, not sure if he should go on; glad to see Aaradhya walking back to the table with a tray.

Janani shook her head, refusing to be cowed down by the feeling of sadness that swept over her. "Let's talk about you and Aaradhya," she said, eyeing her niece's blushing face. "I hear that you guys are pretty close."

Advik grinned, taking Aaradhya's hand in his. "That's right. We plan to set up a global cuisine restaurant soon."

"So, there's going to be an Iyer-Hegde partnership once more," said Janani with a smile.

"Not just one, Janani *Athai*," said Aaradhya, giving Advik a wink.

"That's right," said Advik, lifting his paper cup in a toast. "To fresh partnerships."

Janani sighed, touching her cup to Advik's and Aaradhya's. Could she hope? But then, that's what she had been doing, all these years, living in hope.

"*Ajja* is getting discharged tomorrow morning," said Advik, sipping from his coffee as they sat at a table in the hospital's cafeteria.

Aaradhya gave him a sunny smile. "That's lovely. How is he now?"

Advik shrugged. "Better than before, definitely. But it's a long road to recovery." It was an effort to keep his drooping lips straight.

"He's come this far, Advik. I'm sure he'll be fine."

Advik sighed. "That's what Paritosh Uncle says." He lifted his gaze to hers. "The problem with *Ajja* is that he's such a control freak. I feel that his body simply gave out because of this nature. You know, it simply usurped the control away from him before collapsing."

Aaradhya placed her hand on his as it lay on the table. "I think you should forgive him. He's an old man…"

"Damn it! I'm aware he's old and of course, I've forgiven him. Or I wouldn't be here, would I?" It was an effort not to shout, but Advik managed to keep his voice low. After all, they were still on the hospital premises. But that didn't stop his temper from roiling. After all, it had been so many years since he had lost touch with his grandfather. Forced to keep away, actually.

Aaradhya didn't reply, not keen to aggravate him. It was obvious that Advik was angry, though she wasn't clear as to why. After all, the past was gone and now he was in touch with both his grandparents. He was even back to living in the family home. She didn't realise that his black temper was mainly because Advik continued to feel guilty.

Advik blamed himself for not being at the family home when his grandfather came down with the stroke. However much his father had told him that he shouldn't hold himself responsible, Advik couldn't help it. Maybe he shouldn't have left everything until the last minute all those years ago. He should have told his grandfather that he had been planning to study in the USA way before, preparing him for the event. Instead of informing him only a week before he left home.

He didn't say anything to Aaradhya. She would not understand. How could she? She was her grandfather's pet and had all the freedom in the world, to do exactly what she wanted. Ramani Iyer never placed any kind of restrictions on his children or grandchildren. Advik had been surprised to find out that Aaradhya's cousins, both of them, were working with MNCs in some foreign countries. Imagine that! Madras Meals was a thriving restaurant and made as much money as Mysuru Ahara, if not more. Despite that, the third-generation male members had chosen to take up separate careers, which had nothing to do with the family business.

And look at his Kartik Uncle! The man had remained a bachelor until the age of forty-five, all because of his own father. Damn it all! Advik was torn between the boiling anger and the deep affection he felt for his grandfather. And he couldn't stop mentally beating himself up for staying away. What would have happened if he had gone into the family home after returning from abroad? There would have been angry words. What more? He could have accepted that, right? Why keep away just because he had been told to do so?

Aaradhya looked at the man she was in love with, a soft smile on her face. Despite the angry frown, he looked so handsome, his dimples having disappeared over the past couple of weeks, under the scraggly beard that he hadn't bothered to shave. He also smiled less nowadays, what with his grandfather lying ill in the hospital. The thick fuzz which had joined hands with his handlebar moustache, made him appear rough. Advik of the rugged good looks! She bit her lip to stop herself from smiling, but her eyes gave her away.

"What's funny?" he grumbled, getting up to walk out of the café with her at his side.

"Not funny funny, but cute funny. You look so damn cute with all that fuzz on your cheeks."

"You wanna feel it all over your skin, do you?" he growled, the expression in his eyes suddenly turning sultry and hot.

Colour swept up Aaradhya's face as she stopped in her tracks to stare up into his face. "Don't make promises which you can't keep," she protested.

"Kartik *Chitthaiya* is coming over for a couple of hours to keep *Ajja* company. And I don't have to go to work today."

"Advik…" She shook her head in wonder, her eyes shining.

"And my apartment is only a five-minute car ride."

"This is a damn tempting offer."

"Are you taking it?" he asked, tilting his head to one side to give her a mischievous smile.

"Try and stop me!" She hooked her arm in his as they walked towards the lift.

Kartik reached the elevator bank at the same time. "Hello, lovebirds!" he greeted them with a wide smile, hugging the two of them in turn.

"Hello, Kartik *Chitthaiya*! Hope you are well." Aaradhya grinned at Advik's bachelor uncle with whom she got along like a house on fire. She could see why her aunt, Janani, was still in love with the man.

"I am, my dear, I am. I need a favour from you," said Kartik, his tongue firmly tucked in his cheek even as his eyes danced with mischief.

"Ask away," said Aaradhya.

"Please take this fellow off my hands for some time, will you? He's walking around like a bear with a sore head and I really have no patience for it."

Aaradhya burst out laughing, giving him a vigorous nod.

"Hello! Don't you dare discuss me as if I am not there." Advik shook a finger in his uncle's face.

"Ouch!" Kartik pretended to jump back. "Brat! You are here. I didn't notice."

Aaradhya was bent over double, laughing her head off as Advik took a mock threatening step towards his uncle. "I see what you mean, *Chitthaiya*! I can help you here. Let me take him away so that you can spend some peaceful time with your father," she assured Kartik once she recovered from her laughing bout.

Kartik grimaced. "Thanks, I think!"

It was Advik's turn to laugh out loud, wagging a finger at his uncle. "Serve you right, *Chitthaiya*. You enjoy yourself and I'll see you when I return."

"Don't rush back on my account. I don't mind chilling in the AC room with my feet up. I even have a book to read." Kartik winked at his nephew before waving to them even as the lift door slid closed.

Aaradhya hooked her arm through Advik's, her heart thudding away in her chest at the thought that they were going to spend some private time after so long. And Advik could really do with some pampering, she felt.

They took her car, Advik sliding into the passenger seat, staring dejectedly in front of him. It wasn't long before Aaradhya drove into the car park of his building. Was she glad that he had still retained the apartment despite having shifted to his family home!

They went up to his apartment, Advik opening the door to step inside. He suddenly turned around to push her against the wall, burying his face in her scented neck. "I need you, babe."

She threw her arms around his waist and held on for dear life. Being in his arms after so long was heaven and she had a sneaky feeling that she might melt into a puddle right there in the hallway. She moaned when she felt the brush of his facial hair on her sensitive skin as he nibbled at her collarbone. "Advik…"

He lifted his face to look down at her, tilting her chin with a hand before pressing his lips to hers in a prolonged kiss, his tongue stroking against hers, creating a drugging effect on her senses. It was a long time before he lifted his head to stare at her once again, a small smile stretching his mouth as he took in her reddened and swollen lips. "You look so beautiful," he said, his voice a hoarse whisper. "Come." He took her hand in his and walked towards his bedroom.

They helped undress one another before falling down on the bed, their hands avidly exploring each other's bodies. "You've lost weight," she said, her hands running over his chest, shoulders and arms.

"Hmm…" He didn't give a damn about it, fully aware that he had missed many meals in the past few weeks. "Do you find that repulsive?" he asked, taking a bite of her slender shoulder before working his way down to a luscious breast, drawing a damp tongue over the turgid tip.

"Never," she gasped, her hands clutching his head as she held him close to her body, feeling the pleasurable sensation all the way inside her womb. "Aah!" She rose up in an arc as he closed his lips over the nipple, suckling it deeply. "I love it, Advik."

He ran his hands down the sides of her body, cupping them round her bottom even as he pulled her close to his tumultuous organ. "You taste so damn good, babe," he said, working his way across her chest to the other breast, giving it the same attention.

She mewled, moving restlessly under the onslaught of his hands and mouth, her own running through his hair. She gasped some more when he suddenly removed his mouth from her breast to brush his beard over the sensitive nipple. "Aaaah!"

"Like it?" he asked, laughing softly when he saw the colour rush over her upper body. "I think you do," he answered his own question, bending down to repeat his gesture.

Her head fell back on the pillow, her legs thrashing wildly as she trembled in his arms when Advik teased the sensitive peaks repeatedly. "I lurrvve it," she moaned.

He reached down a hand to cup her femininity even as he opened his mouth to nibble on one tip, soothing it with his tongue when she panted in excitement, her hands clutching his wide shoulders, her nails digging into his flesh.

She crossed her legs, trapping his hand against her body, moaning when she felt his finger sliding into her wetness. "Oh yes!" she moaned some more, lifting her bottom from the bed to press herself against his exploring hand.

He smiled against her breast as he added a second finger down below, making her moan all the louder.

"I want you, Advik, inside me," she demanded, opening her slumberous gaze to meet his heated one.

"Soon," he promised, before moving down the front of her body to press damp kisses under her breasts and over her abdomen. All the while, his fingers continued to stroke her core, bringing her to the brink of an orgasm, but not quite.

"You are torturing me," she protested, her fingers digging into his muscular shoulders. "And you're moving further and further away…"

"Complaints, complaints," he teased, laughing before burying his face in the triangular thatch of hair between her legs.

Aaradhya not only forgot to protest, but actually lost her voice as multiple sensations bombarded her. His beard brushed at the sensitive skin of her inner thighs, making them tremble under the caress. But it was his wicked mouth that undid her as he kissed the lips of her vagina, tracing his tongue over the soft skin before pushing it in, stroking deep within the cavity.

Aaradhya choked, her eyes shutting automatically as she thrilled to his lovemaking, a feeling of rush building deep inside her abdomen. She tried to move her limbs, only to find her thighs trapped by his large hands which kept her pinned to the bed. Her fingers fisting over the bedspread, she could feel the tumult in her lower body building higher and higher, but was unable to do anything about it. It wasn't long before she lost control of herself as an orgasm gushed from within, throwing her up into space, where she felt herself orbiting around the sun along with the other planets. She was totally unaware of her vocal cords coming to life when she shouted in triumph as the feeling of being worshipped overwhelmed her.

Advik lifted his head to gaze at her, a smile of deep satisfaction on his face when he heard her scream. He rose to move up her body to lie down at her side. "Happy?" he asked.

"Too much," she managed to whisper, taking deep breaths to gather some energy. After all, he hadn't reached his climax. "But you..."

"All in time," he said, gathering her in his arms to run a soothing hand over her silky back.

"Mmm..." She buried her face in his chest, even as she slid a hand down his front to take his tumescent manhood in it. "You are... you are..." she mumbled against his chest.

"What?" He tugged her hair to move her face away from him to meet her glowing gaze, an amused expression in his own.

"You are hard."

"That I am," he said, turning on his back to lie down on the bed, his hands stacked under his head.

"Do you want me to...?" She gave him an adoring glance.

"Only if you want to," he said.

With a determined thrust to her chin, she got up to slide down his body, grinning when she heard his loud groan before kneeling between his legs, her hands on his muscular thighs. Leaning forward, she kissed his twitching shaft.

He reached forward to move her tumbling hair out of the way. "I wanna watch," he said.

Sitting back on her heels, she gathered the length of her hair to knot it at the back of her neck before leaning towards him once again. This time, she took his penis in both her hands, caressing him from the root to the tip. Bending down, she kissed the tip before drawing it within her mouth and sucking on it.

"Aaraaaaaaaaaa… you're going to kill me," he groaned, his face drawn as if he was in pain.

"Am I hurting you?" she asked, giving him a mischievous grin as she was only too aware that she was anything but.

He gave her a mock glare. "Enough of this torture, babe. Take me inside you. Come here," he said, when he saw the blank look on her face. When she moved closer, he drew her legs on both sides of his hips, reaching for her vagina to test it with a finger, thrilled to find it wet. He lifted his lower body above the bed and thrust into her, groaning joyously at the way she fitted around him, like a velvet sheath. And the dance began, as old as time, he pulling out to push once again into her. Catching on to the rhythm, Aaradhya rode him, her head thrown back in ecstasy, her chin thrust out in determination as she once again reached out for the pinnacle, her breasts bouncing up and down along with her movements. Advik cupped the twin mounds in his hands and squeezed them gently, his palms rubbing against the tight nubs, making her tremble. "Come on, babe, come for me," he said, his voice hoarse with the effort of holding back his own orgasm as he gritted his teeth, sweat beading on his forehead with the effort.

She whimpered when it burst forth once again, her juices draining out of her before she collapsed on him, totally spent. She moved like a ragdoll when he continued to pound into her a few more times before finding his own release.

"Oh babe!"

19

Kartik had a soft smile on his face as he gazed at the paintings. He always visited every art exhibition of Janani's. Only after making sure that she was nowhere in the vicinity. He spent a lot of time studying each one of them, his eyes taking in every stroke of her paint brush. He couldn't help visualising her at her easel, working on each one.

With his father settled back at home with a round-the-clock nurse and a physiotherapist who visited him daily, Kartik had decided to visit the art gallery in South Bombay after the lunch hour rush was over at Mysuru Ahara. There was no one in the gallery except for one caretaker, the crowd usually showing up after five in the evenings.

He had been thinking a lot nowadays, seriously considering his nephew's advice. Advik had repeatedly told Kartik that he should not compromise on his own life, just because his parents thought differently.

"You have only one life, *Chitthaiya*. And you should live it to the full. What's the use of blaming anyone after leading an unhappy life? Aaradhya's aunt is also unhappy, leading a single life. Do you realise that it's in your hands? Yours and Janani *Athai's* happiness?"

"Have you met her?" asked Kartik, staring at his nephew.

Advik nodded. "Yes, I did. Aaradhya brought her over to meet me."

"Oh! You never told me!" Kartik accused his nephew.

"I'm doing exactly that now, aren't I?"

Kartik couldn't come up with a suitable reply to that. "How is she?" he asked.

"Who?" Advik lifted an eyebrow, giving his uncle a sly glance.

"Janani. Who else?"

"Janani *Athai* seems all fine on the surface. But deep down she pines for you, *Chitthaiya*. I couldn't miss the sadness behind her smile. Especially when she saw me. She says I look exactly like you."

"She did that?" There was a look of deep longing on Kartik's face when he asked the question. He felt envious of his nephew who had recently met Janani.

"Yes! But *Chitthaiya,* tell me something…" Advik paused, a mischievous smile on his face.

Kartik shook his head to clear it before giving his nephew his complete attention. "What?"

"Do I look so ugly?" asked Advik, looking completely serious.

"What? I don't get you." Kartik frowned at his nephew.

"Well, Janani *Athai* said that I resemble you a lot. That's why…"

Kartik lifted a hand as if to slap his nephew who burst out laughing. "You *na, Chitthaiya,* are madly in love with the lady. I really don't understand why you are torturing yourself like this."

Kartik pulled himself back to the present as he looked around the gallery to check out Janani's art work.

There were twenty-five paintings in all and some of them already had a small sticker on it stating that the piece was sold. His eyes went to the one with a peacock in the middle of the forest, a soft sigh escaping him as he gazed at it avidly. It also had a 'sold' sticker on it. Uncaring, he studied the play of light and shadow on the painting. The colours were simply brilliant, the dark green foliage forming the perfect background to the bird which was on the verge of spreading its plumage. It seemed as if it would open up its feathers fully at any moment, so much so that it appeared totally real. Ignoring the sign that said 'do not touch', he reached a finger to run it over the partly opened tail feathers, visualising Janani's paint brush creating the strokes.

"Ahem!"

He turned around in a flash when he heard the sound, his mouth falling open when he saw the artist herself standing in front of him, a soft smile on her beautiful face. He blinked a couple of times, as if to make sure that she wasn't a figment of his imagination. "Janu..."

"The one and only. What are you doing here, Kartik?" she asked, staring at his handsome face, the years falling away as they looked into each other's eyes, their hearts picking up pace to thud away in their rib cages, their breaths coming in gasps.

"I..." He stopped, took a deep breath and straightened his shoulders before continuing. After all, he wasn't exactly committing a sin, was he? He was a collector of her paintings and as her customer, he had every right to visit her exhibition. "I came to check out the paintings."

"Oh! Did you know they were mine?" she asked, her heart in her throat, her eyes filming over with a trace of unshed tears. She took in the strands of white hair which were woven along with the black ones on Kartik's head. Otherwise, he didn't look all that different. Okay, he had put on some weight, but then in those days, Kartik used to be reed thin. She recalled the night she had spent in his arms and a fiery blush bloomed on her cheeks.

On the verge of answering her question, he shut his mouth when he noticed the sudden colour flaring on her cheeks. He couldn't help the small smile that sprouted on his face as he immediately realised what she was thinking about. "I've missed you Janu."

"Are you sure?" she asked, standing straight, challenge in her stance. Drawing a deep breath, she willed the colour to leave her face. No, she wasn't going to let him off so easily. How could she? The way she missed him day in and day out.

"As sure as there's breath in my body," he said, his voice a soft whisper as he stepped nearer to her. He needed to get closer to her warmth. Or he might go mad with the longing that tore at him; through him.

"But you still haven't bothered to do anything about it," she accused, unable to take her gaze away from his. She couldn't help seeing the love shining in it. It was an effort not to throw herself into his arms and let the rest of the world simply go to hell.

"Janu..." He was so glad that there was not a single soul in the art gallery other than the two of them. The person manning the counter had gone, probably for a tea break. He didn't really care. What he cared about was the fact that he was meeting the love of his life after twenty-three years. Imagine that! His mouth drooped at the corners. And they both lived in the same city too.

"Kartik..." She reached across to run her thumb over his lips, applying pressure to one edge, as if she was trying to make him smile.

He couldn't help but smile, his eyes closing of their own volition as he experienced her searing touch, that too on his lips. "My love..." he breathed, kissing the pad of her thumb.

And just like that, she was in his arms. Kartik didn't quite know what came over him as he gathered her close to his chest. Maybe it was the fact that his father wasn't as powerful as he had imagined. After all, the patriarch was sick and in bed nowadays. And maybe it was his nephew's repeated advice, that Kartik should get back with the woman he loved. Or maybe it was getting to know Aaradhya, who was the spit image of her aunt Janani—the woman he had held a candle to all his life. Whatever the reason, he was simply glad that they were together today.

"I never stopped loving you, Janu," he told her in a hoarse whisper when they came up for air. The kiss was as sweet as he remembered, maybe even better than before.

"Nor have I stopped loving you," she said, reaching forward to kiss his cheek.

"Marry me!"

She gave a startled shout of laughter. "Are you sure?" she asked, lifting a challenging eyebrow.

"Yes. After all these years, I realise that my father doesn't matter; nor does my mother. It is you who I need at my side."

Tears welled up in Janani's eyes before one quietly rolled down her left cheek. "I don't want to make enemies of them, not after waiting this long," she averred.

He gave a guttural laugh. "You mean they were your friends all these years?" he asked sarcastically.

She smiled through her tears. "Not me, idiot. I don't want them to become your enemies." She punched his shoulder with a small fist.

He covered her fist with his large hand before lifting it to his lips, his eyes devouring her. "If they have a bit of sense in them, they wouldn't make an enemy out of me." His confidence had grown as he watched his nephew over the past few weeks. While Advik adored his family members and treated each one of them with respect, he was absolutely sure of his goals and went after them.

Advik's maxim: *It's my life and I want to live it to the full. As long as I don't hurt anyone. But if their ego comes in the way, it's their problem, not mine.*

So simple, so sensible, so mature!

Kartik quickly explained to Janani about his sudden change of mind.

A frown pleated her eyebrows. "But I don't understand. Why didn't you seek me out immediately?"

He gave her a wide grin. "The change occurred only these past couple of weeks. You know, my father had a paralytic stroke and was hospitalised. Before that, he had thrown my nephew out of the family home..." He told her the whole story of how Advik was back in the fold. "I have been observing Advik's behaviour, how he interacts with my parents. You know, the boy is adorable, but firm. He doesn't buckle under their pressure."

Janani smiled, leaning her head on his shoulder, her arms around his waist. "You know something, I think Aaradhya is extremely lucky to have fallen for your Advik. Before you ask, my niece introduced the two of us."

He tilted her chin to look deeply into her eyes. "Should I feel jealous?" he asked outright.

She burst out laughing. "Of what? That I think highly of Advik? Don't be silly. It's you I love, Kartik. Always!" Her eyes turned serious as she lifted a hand to cup his cheek. "I'll marry you whenever you say."

He kissed her forehead. "Thank you, my love. I am truly honoured. I would like to meet Ramani Uncle to begin with. I need to apologise to him first before seeking his blessings. Do you think he'll forgive me?" he asked. He knew that if it were his father, Bhaskar wouldn't be so forgiving.

Janani smiled, tracing her thumb once again over his mouth, finding him irresistible. "There is no question of forgiveness, Kartik. My father was never angry with you in the first place."

He buried his face in her crook of her neck, his body shuddering with fluctuating emotions.

Janani ran her hand soothingly over his head, giving him time to calm down as she felt the dampness of his tears on her skin. It was a while before she said, "Don't, my love. The past is all gone; done and dusted. But the present and future are ours. Don't you think we should celebrate instead of feeling sad?"

He took a deep breath to calm down, lifting his head to smile at her through his tears. Taking a handkerchief from his pants pocket, he wiped his face before blowing his nose. "You are right, Janu, as always. I only wish I had the sense…"

She stopped him mid-sentence, a hand over his mouth as she shook her head. "Now, today! I want you."

Colour ran up his rugged face as he met her bold gaze. She hadn't changed one little bit, his Janani.

"Come with me," she said, taking his hand in hers.

"Where are we going?" he asked, dazed.

"My apartment."

"Your parents?"

"I live alone. You can meet everyone afterwards. For now, you are mine."

He just sat there in the passenger seat of her car, turned sideways to gaze at her as she navigated the Mumbai traffic efficiently. "I adore you, Janu."

"I know," she said, giving him a mischievous glance from the corner of her eyes. "Why do you think I have waited for you all these years?"

A deep sigh shuddered its way out of his chest. But Kartik didn't utter a word. No, she was right! There was no sense speaking about the past, the time lost. He was going to live for the present.

"Can I come to live with you just in case my parents throw me out of my home?"

"Hahaha! You know you are welcome. You don't even have to wait for them to throw you out. Anyway, can you imagine me living in your home with your parents when we are married?"

There was a startled expression on his face which made it obvious that he hadn't thought about the practicalities of the situation. And no, she would never fit in the Hegde household, not with his mother and father. He suddenly wondered how his brother's wife, Vrunda, got along with Bhaskar and Akshatha and felt rather sorry for his sister-in-law.

Janani laughed some more. "I think you should close your mouth, just in case a fly plans to take residence there," she teased. "You will have to live with me even if your parents don't throw you out. I have a big enough apartment and it's close to your place of work. As for me, I have a studio set up in the flat."

"Hmm… sounds good." Things were moving a little too fast for him. But then, it was he who had suggested that they get married. "I…"

She placed a hand on his thigh, making him go hard with need. "You shouldn't worry, Kartik. Let's take it one day at a time, shall we?"

His scowl vanished to be replaced by a smile. "Okay, my love."

From now on, Kartik was ready to walk to the end of the earth if it was Janani who invited him.

20

"Where are you *Chitthaiya*? I haven't seen you in ages," asked Advik, typing quickly on his laptop while he attended Kartik's phone call. He was sitting in his office cabin at an Indian restaurant in Phoenix Market City. He had not seen his uncle for four days. Nor had he heard from him. His father had mentioned something about Kartik being on a break.

Kartik laughed. "I've been in heaven, my boy, in heaven."

Advik stopped typing to focus on the conversation. He had never heard this kind of enthusiasm—any kind of enthusiasm for that matter—in his uncle's voice. "What's up, *Chitthaiya*? Tell me all."

Kartik laughed some more. "I'm married."

Advik shot out of his office chair as if it had caught fire. "What? Don't tell me. Who's the lucky woman?" His uncle had not married all these years because he was supposedly in love with Janani Iyer. Advik had even met the lady, and told her how much his uncle still loved her. And now his uncle says he was suddenly married. To whom?

"Janani Iyer Hegde! The woman I have always loved," said Kartik, a jubilant note in his voice.

"This is simply fantastic! But how, when? Why did you not tell me anything? I would have…"

"Wait! Wait! I met Janani four days ago, quite by chance. That's when I realised that I never wanted to live without her in my life. We decided to get married. Her father was totally encouraging and we got married yesterday. Right now, we are at the airport, catching a flight to Maldives, for our honeymoon."

Advik threw back his head and laughed out ecstatically. "You are a deep one, *Chitthaiya*. And I am so, so thrilled for you. I can't wait to tell Aara. She'll be so excited. I…"

"Janu is speaking to your Aara right now," said Kartik. "And listen, brat. I have to thank *you* for everything. This was possible only because of you."

"Me? But how?" Advik was genuinely surprised.

"I've been watching you, brat. I even told Janani about it. How you love everyone, but kowtow to none. It's a life lesson I have learnt from you." His voice had turned shaky with emotion by now. "And I've also been listening to the lectures you've been giving me. It's only because of all that I had the guts to propose to Janani."

"Aww *Chitthaiya*! This is totally unexpected. But I am glad if I have been of help. And congratulations! I wish you both a wonderful life. By the way, does *Appa* know?"

"I had to call you first, Advik. I'm planning to call Ganesh immediately after."

Advik was totally touched. He wished his uncle once again before Kartik disconnected the call.

It was late when Advik reached home, to find his parents sitting in the living room. He missed spending time with Aaradhya during the nights. But then, with his grandfather installed back in the family home, it didn't make sense to retain his rented flat. And they did manage to sneak to her terrace some times to spend some private time as they lounged around the private swimming pool.

"Do you know?" asked Vrunda, the moment Advik stepped inside the house.

"About *Chitthaiya's* marriage? Yes, he phoned me from the airport."

"I still can't believe Kartik has actually done it." Ganesh shook his head, dazed. Not that he was angry with his brother or anything like that. Just stunned that Kartik was capable of taking such a bold decision. "And not a word to anybody too."

Advik grinned, going to sit on the arm of the sofa, next to his father. "Dad! It's high time *Chitthaiya* married Janani *Athai*. And it can't be at a better time. *Ajja* seems in a highly forgiving mood nowadays." Which was the truth. Bhaskar's ego had taken quite a toss because of the illness that had made him go silent. He also could see the way his family rallied around him, especially his grandson. He had been touched by the way Advik had insisted on spending every moment at his bedside, until he was surely on the road to recovery. All this, after he had shunned the boy, so terribly too.

Ganesh gave his son a curious look when he heard the term '*Athai*' before giving a shrug. "You could be right. And by the way, Ramani Uncle called me today. He wants to meet *Appa*." There was a worried frown on his face.

"I hope you invited him over," said Advik, looking at his mother before returning his gaze to his father.

"Of course he did, Advik. How could he not? Ramani Uncle is such an honourable man. If he could stoop down low enough to connect with us, we should also be nice to him, no?" Vrunda spoke rapidly. The two of them were a mite worried about Akshatha's reaction though.

"Does *Ajji* know about this?" Advik came straight to the crux of the matter.

Ganesh sighed, long and loud. "I haven't told her anything yet."

"When is Ramani *Thatha* coming?"

Vrunda gave her son a surprised glance. First it was *Athai*. And now it was *Thatha*! Wasn't that the word for grandfather in Tamil?

"Tomorrow morning. I invited him for breakfast." It was Ganesh who replied.

"That's really nice of you, Dad. Do you want me to speak to *Ajji*?" He almost laughed out loud when he saw a similar expression of relief on both his parents' faces. "Don't worry. I'll take care of the matter."

"Tell me something, Advik. How come you call Ramani Uncle *Thatha*?" Vrunda asked her son.

A trace of colour ran up his cheeks as Advik met his mother's curious gaze. But Ganesh spoke before his son could respond. "And you also called Janani *Athai*. Is it something to do with Aaradhya Iyer's influence?" he asked his son.

"Huh?" Advik's eyes went wide as he looked at his father in surprise. "Do you know Aaradhya?"

It was Ganesh's turn to grin. "I don't know the young lady, exactly. But I have met her. She's the spit image of her aunt, Janani. Do you know her well?"

Vrunda looked from one man to the other, listening to them without interrupting.

In the biblical sense! Advik didn't utter the words that sprang to his mind. Taking a deep breath, he said, "You can say that. Er... Dad, Mom, I am in love with Aaradhya. And would like to marry her sometime in the future. Maybe after five or six years."

Ganesh frowned. "What's wrong with this year? I know that your *Ajja* and *Ajji* might have some objections. But I am all for the match as Aaradhya is Ramani Uncle's granddaughter. At twenty-eight, you aren't really young, Advik." He turned to his wife to see if she was in agreement.

Vrunda smiled through her tears. Her son was in love, and wanted to get married, finally. And she agreed with her husband. If the girl was Ramani Uncle's granddaughter, she didn't need any other recommendation. "Your *Appa* is right, Advik. You aren't growing younger. And I am sure Aaradhya's family will also want her to get married soon."

Advik slid down to his knees in front of his parents, his hands on their knees. "Listen, guys. You both are from the old millennium and prefer to live your lives differently. Aaradhya and I are both interested in setting up our careers; and need time for it. You will have to please understand our point of view."

Ganesh stared at his son, a thoughtful expression on his face. Advik was smart, intelligent and hardworking. More than all that, he was a loving son and a grandson. Even he had been surprised at the way Advik had taken care of his sick grandfather, with not a bit of rancour for the way the old man had treated him. The fact was that his son had his head firmly screwed on his shoulders.

And now, according to Kartik, it was thanks to Advik's advice that he was married to the woman he loved, after all these years. Ganesh finally arrived at the conclusion that more than anything else, his son was wise.

Placing a hand on his son's shoulder, he said, "Whatever you wish, my son. I will not stand in your way. And I will always love you, whatever you do."

"You are the best, Dad." Advik got up to hug his father, drawing his mother into the fold. "Mom?"

Vrunda sniffed. She wasn't at all sure that she agreed with her husband, but she accepted that he knew best. "Whatever *Appa* says, Advik. As long as you are happy."

"Now that's sorted, let me go speak to *Ajji* regarding Ramani *Thatha's* visit tomorrow." He knew that Akshatha slept late and was probably sitting next to his grandfather, watching TV.

Ganesh and Vrunda held each other's hands tightly when they heard the shouting from the upper floor. It was his mother, screaming at the top of her voice, notwithstanding the fact that her husband was still not completely recovered yet, almost a month after he suffered the stroke.

Akshatha was jumping up and down despite her excess weight, her eyes sparking flame at her grandson. Talk about killing the messenger!

"How dare you bring such terrible news to me, Advik? How dare you? If that Iyer man does not have any shame, that's his business. But you are a Hegde. How can you agree to his coming to our home? It's been over thirty years and we have never felt the need to connect with that family. Why now?" She paused to take deep breaths, clutching her heaving chest.

"*Ajji!* Will you please calm down?" said Advik in a firm voice. "I think *Ajja* is getting agitated with all that shouting."

On the verge of responding to her grandson with a cutting reply, Akshatha noticed her husband who was shaking his left hand wildly, even as growling sounds emanated from his throat. Visibly calming down, she went across to his side and took his hand in hers.

Bhaskar ignored her, his gaze steady on his grandson. Pulling his hand out of his wife's hold, he gestured to Advik to step closer to him.

"*Ajja!* I am sorry for upsetting you. But I thought it best that Ramani *Thatha's* visit doesn't spring as a surprise. Please *Ajja*! This enmity has lasted for too damn long. If the Iyer patriarch is keen to visit us, why not welcome him? If you ask me, I think your friend is worried about your health. I am sure he wants to see for himself that you are recovering well."

Tears sprung into Bhaskar's eyes and fell down into the pillow. He took his grandson's hand and pressed it firmly, indicating that he welcomed the idea. Over the past weeks, grandfather and grandson had arrived at a way of communicating which was working well for the both of them.

Advik smiled at his grandfather. "I think you are happy to meet your long-lost friend."

Bhaskar shut his eyes in a gesture of agreement before opening them once again.

"But how? Why now? I am sure the man's coming over to gloat over your illness. He…"

Bhaskar effectively stopped his wife from speaking further by slapping her hand with his, much to her shock.

"Alright. You all do what you want. What respect do I have in this house anyway?" Muttering loudly, Akshatha walked into the adjoining dressing room and shut herself there.

Bhaskar gave his grandson a lopsided smile, pressing his hand once again.

"I think you should go to sleep, *Ajja*. You must be tired."

Bhaskar patted the side of his bed, indicating that Advik should sit next to him. He gestured with his left hand to ask if there was anything else he wanted to say.

Advik hesitated only for a moment before speaking. "There is another news, *Ajja*. I believe it's happy news. But I am not so sure about you. Anyway,

Kartik *Chitthaiya* married Janani Iyer in a secret ceremony yesterday." Advik was well aware that his father wouldn't thank him if Bhaskar suffered another stroke and died as a consequence.

More tears welled up in Bhaskar's eyes as he lifted his hand to place it on Advik's shoulder, giving a tiny nod which was the most he could manage.

"I am glad, *Ajja*. I am so glad that you have no objection to it. Kartik *Chitthaiya* deserves to be happy." He chatted some more, telling his grandfather about his day at work, about Chinese cuisine and the ingredients that went into it. As always, listening about food and different recipes made Bhaskar's eyes light up. It was a long while before his eyelids fluttered shut as sleep finally claimed him.

Advik got up from the bed, nodded to the nurse who had been sitting quietly in a corner, and left his grandfather's bedroom. He knocked on his parents' room and told them that the deed was done.

"But your *Ajji* was shouting…?" Ganesh asked, a worried frown on his forehead.

Advik shrugged. "She's angry, yes. But *Ajja* has accepted the situation. And he's even looking forward to his friend's visit. And by the way, I told *Ajja* about Kartik *Chitthaiya's* marriage."

Vrunda's eyes went wide with shock. "But…"

"It's okay, Mom. *Ajja* took it in his stride. It's better that he knows about the wedding before Ramani *Thatha* comes tomorrow."

Ganesh shook his head at his son, but the smile refused to leave his face. Advik had achieved way more in one night than what he and Kartik hadn't been able to achieve in thirty years. "Good for you, son."

"Thanks Dad. And good night, you both. I'm off to bed. See you guys in the morning."

He went to his room to pull out his phone to type quickly into the Tinder app chat box.

Hey, babe. Sorry couldn't get away before now. Was chatting with Ajja. I just wanted to tell you how much I love you.

He added a heart emoji to the message before hitting send and wasn't really surprised when his phone rang almost immediately.

"How much?" Aaradhya's voice was a whisper in his ear, but he still didn't miss the smile in her voice.

"Huh?"

"How much do you love me?"

"Hmm… let me see…" Advik paused, a grin on his face as he stepped out of his shoes before removing his belt.

"Advik!"

"Wait, babe. I need to think…" He switched the speaker button on his phone to get out of his work clothes. "Shall I call you later? I need a shower."

"I am wondering if I should come over and throttle you with both my hands!" Aaradhya grumbled, lying back on her bed, grinning from ear to ear.

"I can definitely find better work for your hands. You know…"

"Advik!" She shouted over the phone, making him laugh. "Are you even going to tell me?"

"I adore you, Aara. And love you more than life itself," he responded, placing the phone once again against his ear.

"Awww… that's so sweet of you."

"So, are you going to tell me?"

"What?"

"How much do you love me?"

"Who told you that I love you?" she asked, giggling uncontrollably.

"Should I come over to your terrace and ask you in person?"

"It's almost two. And listen, shall I come along with *Thatha* tomorrow?"

"I was sure you would," he said, laughing. "After all, you must be missing me terribly, not having seen me for almost twenty-four hours."

"Meh! I dare you to kiss me when I visit you," she challenged.

"You are on."

They chatted for a bit longer before disconnecting. It was no surprise that sleep took a long time coming to the lovers who were too far apart from one another.

21

Ramani held his granddaughter's hand tightly in his when they waited for someone to open the door to the Hegdes' duplex flat. He couldn't deny to being a tad nervous about meeting his old friend. And he was also worried for Bhaskar's health. It was only the earlier day when he had got to know about his friend's stroke. In fact, he had scolded Aaradhya for keeping the information away from him.

Advik opened the door with a broad smile. "Welcome, welcome, Ramani *Thatha*." He bent down to touch the older man's feet once he crossed the threshold into the living room. "And hello Aara."

"You must be Advik. I am glad to finally make your acquaintance," said Ramani, smiling at the strapping young man. So! This was the man his granddaughter was in love with. Excellent choice indeed!

"The same goes for me too, *Thatha*. Please come on in. *Appa*..." He stopped when he saw Ganesh coming down the stairs.

"Ramani Uncle!" Ganesh rushed forward to hug the older man. "I'm so, so happy to meet you after all these years. And thank you so much, Uncle. You truly have a big heart, forgiving us..."

"There's nothing to forgive, son." Ramani smiled at his best friend's elder son.

Vrunda came from the kitchen to greet their esteemed guest by touching his feet and welcoming him.

Ramani didn't take the seat he was offered. "I am keen to meet Bhaskar first."

"*Appa's* room is upstairs," said Ganesh, guiding the guest towards the staircase.

Advik snagged Aaradhya's hand, stopping her from following them. Turning to his mother, he said, "Mom, this is Aaradhya. You remember, I spoke to you about her? And Aaradhya, this is my mother, Vrunda."

"Namaste, Vrunda Aunty," said Aaradhya, bringing both her hands together in greeting.

"Hello, my dear. I am so glad to meet you. You must be what...? Twenty years old?"

"Mom!" Advik rolled his eyes at the ceiling.

Aaradhya pressed his hand, stopping him from saying anything further. "I am twenty-three, aunty."

"Why don't you both come into the dining room? You can have your breakfast. Ramani Uncle and Ganesh might prefer to have their breakfast with your *Ajja*."

"Er... Mom. Give us some time, *na*? We'll join you in fifteen, okay? I need to..."

Vrunda gave a nod, implicitly understanding what her son was trying to tell her. "Okay. I'll see you both soon." She did an about turn and went back into the dining area.

"How could you, Advik?" Aaradhya's face was a brilliant shade of red as she glared at him.

Grinning unabashedly, he took her hand and raced up the stairs, dragging her all the way to his room. Shutting the door, he pushed her against it to place his lips on hers and kissed her hungrily.

It was a long time before they broke the kiss, taking deep breaths to calm down their thundering hearts. "I've missed you, Aara." He buried his face in the crook of her neck. "Did I tell you how beautiful you look?"

"More than you?" she asked, hugging him close. "Hey! You can't be so hard, not this early in the morning," she said, her hand rubbing against his lower body.

"Says who?" he growled, nibbling his way along her slender shoulder before kissing her cheek. "You keep doing that and I might just come in your hand."

"Do you wanna try it?" she asked, a shapely eyebrow rising up over half-closed eyes.

He groaned, shaking his head slowly from side to side. "I met your challenge which was only to kiss you in my home. More than that will have to wait."

"Wait until what? When?" she asked, continuing to caress him, her hand moving up and down.

He shuddered, pressing himself closer into her hand. "That feels so good, babe." His groan was louder this time. "Wait until we are married."

"What?" Aaradhya jumped back, removing her hand from his body. "You want me to wait five damn years to make love to you?"

He laughed. "Not that, you idiot! Making love right here in this bedroom is what I am talking about."

She pouted at him. "Why don't we move in together somewhere?"

"Will your family object?" he asked. He wasn't even going to think about what his family was going to say about it.

"I'm sure," she said, tracing a finger over his moustache. "But so what? I'll convince them somehow."

He took her wandering finger into his mouth and bit it gently, making her moan in delight. "It won't be easy. But that's no issue. I think you're right. Let's go house hunting this week then."

"You mean it?" she asked eagerly, pressing close to his chest and snuggling there.

"Yes, I do. I think we should go down now."

She moved away with obvious reluctance. "Okay."

He laughed again. "I hope you will change your expression when we walk into the dining room. Just now, you look as if you are going to your funeral."

"Meh! You know a woman has her needs. And she came hoping…" she yelped when he squeezed her breast, her eyes glazing over. "Advik…"

"Temptress!" He nipped her lower lip before soothing it with his tongue. Wielding a playful slap to her bottom, he said, "Let's go."

Ramani went to sit on the chair on the left side of Bhaskar's bed, not showing the shock he felt, doing his best to keep his face blank of expression. His friend had shrunken so much. It wasn't as if Bhaskar had ever been fat. But right now, he could have passed off for a skeleton, a bag of skin and bones.

"Bhaskar…" Ramani took his left hand in both of his, an overwhelming feeling of love in his heart. Aware that the other man was in no state to speak, he continued to talk. "I know it's not the best of circumstances for us to meet after being away for so long. But I'm so happy to see you, my friend. You know something, Bhaskar, you have always remained my best friend. No one else could even come a close second."

Bhaskar listened, cleansing tears pouring from his eyes, turning his pillow wet. Not that he cared. He was undergoing a major catharsis, his battered ego dissolving little by little on listening to his best friend's loving words.

Akshatha, who had put a foot inside the room, all set to blast the Iyer patriarch, stopped right where she was, listening to Ramani's loving words.

Ramani spoke non-stop, running over the time when they first arrived in Bombay. He recalled many instances of joys, triumphs, achievements and more. "Life has never been the same, Bhaskar, not without you. And you know something, our children have understood that way better than the two of us cranky old men." He paused when he saw Bhaskar smiling for the first time. "That's right, we both are really two cranky old men."

He continued to talk even as breakfast was served, the male nurse feeding Bhaskar one bite after another.

Bhaskar's gaze continued to remain on his friend as he listened to him avidly. He felt a lightness of heart that he hadn't felt in decades, feeling younger all of a sudden.

Ramani visited his friend every day after that, spending precious hours, willing Bhaskar to get out of his sick bed and return to a normal life. It took time, it took patience. But then, Ramani had both, in plenty.

Some might even call it a miracle, but the doctor found terrific improvement in Bhaskar's health over the next few months. Neither grandfather raised an objection when Advik and Aaradhya insisted on moving into a home of their own, giving their whole hearted blessings. After all, they had realised by now that the present generation truly knew the value of 'live and let live' and the older generation decided to simply take a leaf out of their books.

It wasn't long before Madras Meals was transformed into a global cuisine restaurant helmed by both Advik and Aaradhya. They had decided to call it Rambhas, combining the first syllable of the names of their respective grandfathers.

As for the grandmothers—Savitri and Akshatha continued to be wary of each other, but they also decided to keep their peace. After all, Savitri was married to a man who was as rich as Akshatha's husband.

Kumar Iyer—Aaradhya's father—became best friends with Ganesh Hegde—Advik's father. They made elaborate plans for their children's wedding along with their wives, Vaibhavi Iyer and Vrunda Hegde. Vaibhavi and Vrunda didn't have a problem getting along and were extremely enthusiastic about their respective children's lives.

As for Advik and Aaradhya, they were thrilled to build the clientele for their new restaurant, which soon went on to become the pride of Matunga.

I love you, babe!

Aaradhya smiled when she opened the Tinder chat box to see her boyfriend's message.

How much?

Why don't you walk into our office cabin? I'll tell you in person.

She hailed the new manager and ensured that he was taking care of the billing counter before walking to the back of the restaurant. When they had renovated the old restaurant, both she and Advik had made sure that the windows of the office cabin were fitted with one-way mirror instead of glass. After all, they planned to spend a lot of time at work. And a couple needed their privacy, right?

Aaradhya stepped into the office and locked the door behind her. Walking around the desk, she fell into Advik's lap and was thrilled when he threw both his arms around her in a fierce hug. She turned around in his arms to kiss him. "Tell me."

"Hmm…" He kissed her some more, his hands cupping her breasts, his palms rubbing over the tightening nubs.

She pressed herself closer into his hands, nipping his ear before sucking on it. "Tell me."

"Aren't you demanding?" he teased, leaning back in his chair to give her a lazy glance, running his gaze over her upper body. "Did I tell you how sexy you look?" He pinched her left nipple with his right thumb and forefinger, making her moan in ecstacy.

"Tell me more," she said, placing her hand over his to press it closer to her breast.

"Okay, let me see. I love you more than I love Tinder..."

"What?" She jumped up before falling into his lap with a thud.

"Ouch! Easy, woman. You don't plan on making me impotent, do you?" he said, his eyes dancing mischievously.

"Very funny!" she pouted. "What was that about Tinder?"

"Well, it's like this: it was Tinder that brought us together. And that's why I love the app. Let's say I love you way more than that."

"Meh..." He stopped her effectively by kissing her some more.

Aaradhya simply surrendered to his lovemaking. Rambhas will have to take care of itself for a bit longer as she basked in Advik's Tinder Loving Care.

THE END

MORE BOOKS BY SUNDARI VENKATRAMAN

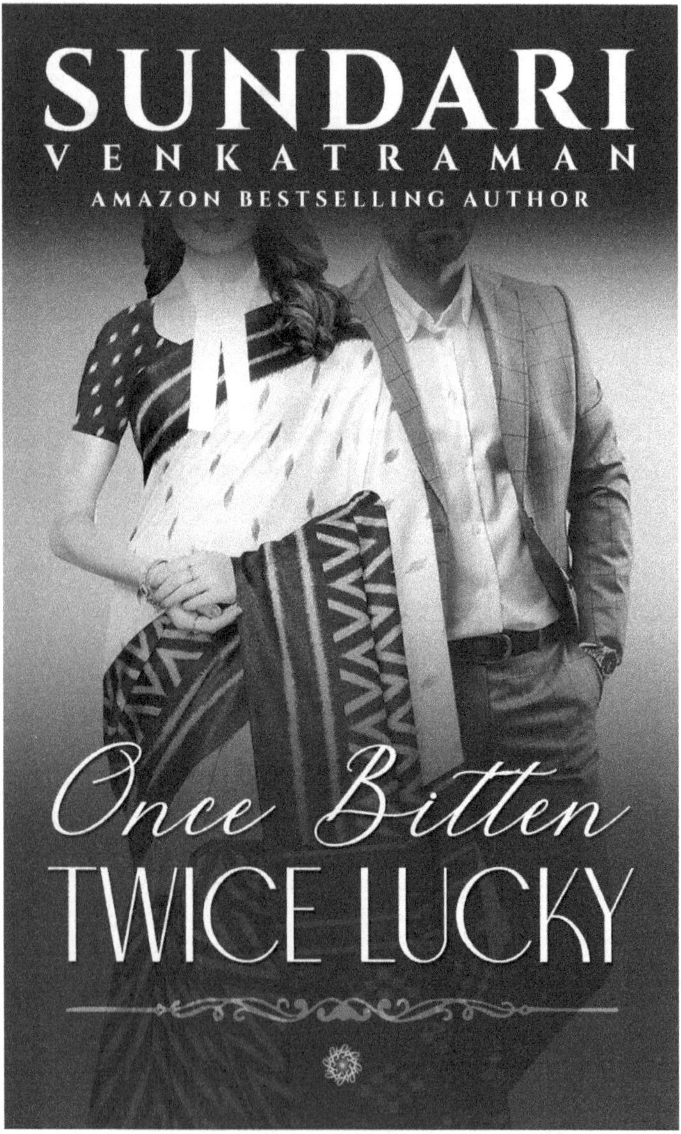
SUNDARI
VENKATRAMAN
AMAZON BESTSELLING AUTHOR
Once Bitten
TWICE LUCKY

Another contemporary romance
by Sundari Venkatraman...
ONCE BITTEN TWICE LUCKY

Deepshika feels as free as a bird once she decides to kick her womaniser husband out of her life. The lawyer is confident of bringing up her teenage kids with her father's help.

Karan isn't all that upset when his wife dumps him, leaving behind their preteen daughter for him to bring up. But the alimony she claims comes as a rude shock.

Sparks fly when the shocked husband meets the divorced, divorce lawyer. But what will happen when their respective children come face to face? Will they accept their parents' relationship or rebel against it?

Will the once bitten Deepshika and Karan be lucky in their relationship the second time?

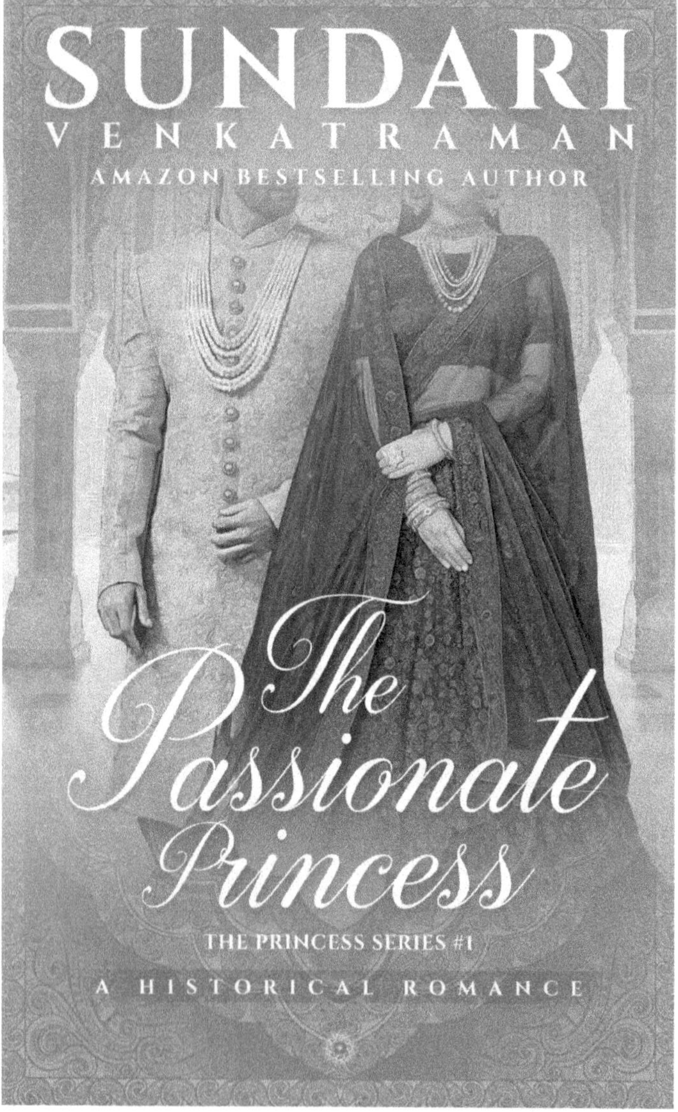
SUNDARI
VENKATRAMAN
AMAZON BESTSELLING AUTHOR
The Passionate Princess
THE PRINCESS SERIES #1
A HISTORICAL ROMANCE

Book #1 from The Princess Series
THE PASSIONATE PRINCESS

All it took was one look. And they were in love... Princess Hemangini is mesmerised by Prince Devendra when she falls into his arms while rushing across the royal gardens.

The Prince of Indrapuri is amazed that the Princess of Mahendrapuri is even more beautiful and graceful than what the visiting bards sang in praise of her.

Their mutual attraction blooms into love and they decide to get married. Tying the knot is easy, but consummating the marriage is another matter altogether.

As their love and passion draw them towards each other, Devendra's mother, Queen Kanchana Devi, keeps throwing obstacles in the path of the lovers; sometimes in the name of rituals and sometimes inflicting doubts in their minds; doing her best to keep them apart.

As the frustrated bride and groom tolerate the intervening time with impatience, something happens to shake up Hemangini; something that makes her refuse to let her husband touch her.

What will the proud prince have to do to make his princess fall into his arms once again?

Read this historical romance from India to find out if the passionate princess finds happiness with her prince or not.

SUNDARI
VENKATRAMAN
AMAZON BESTSELLING AUTHOR
THE Rebel PRINCESS
THE PRINCESS SERIES BOOK 2

Book #2 from The Princess Series
THE REBEL PRINCESS

Having lost her royal parents in a palace fire at the young age of four, Chamundeswari is brought up to be the docile princess of a vassal kingdom by her stepmother who is also the newly crowned queen and her brother, the chief minister.

Though Vijayendran is the youngest born of the Chozha Emperor and his temple dancer wife, he grows up to be a great warrior and leader under the auspices of his elder brother Rajendran only after his father's death. He has been especially trained by the newly crowned king to win over territories and annex them to the greatest empire of those times.

The earth quakes and the skies shiver when Chamundeswari and Vijayendran come face to face. But is everything what it appears to be on the surface? Forget being docile, the princess with a tiger for her pet, appears to be a rebel through and through. And the warrior whose strength is to annex regions could be the very person the princess needs to save her kingdom.

But will The Rebel Princess heed the words of the man who sets her on fire with a mere glance?

Connect with Sundari Venkatraman here:

Sundari Venkatraman Books

Sundari Venkatraman Books

https://www.sundarivenkatraman.in

Author Sundari Venkatraman

@sundarivenkat

@sundarivenkatraman

sundarivenkat@gmail.com

CPSIA information can be obtained
at www.ICGtesting.com
Printed in the USA
LVHW052231021121
702257LV00006B/122